Debris

Debris

Andrew Humphrey

Cover photography by Peter Corr
(www.petercorrart.com)

ISBN number: 978-1-7398195-5-2

Printed and Bound by 4Edge

Published by:

Head Shot
85 Gertrude Road
Norwich
UK

editorheadshot@gmail.com
www.headshotpress.com

I would like to extend my sincere thanks to James Sallis, a writer whom I have for so long admired, for reading *Debris* and kindly providing a quote for the cover, and to Peter Corr, for the use of his excellent photography.

And many thanks, as ever, to Andrew Hook, for his continued support and encouragement.

Chapter 1

My brother's cottage sits at the end of a small terrace. It's surrounded by fenland; spare and flat and bleak. Patrick must have heard my car pull up, as he waits for me at the front door. The day is November cold, the air mist-edged, indifferent and I'm glad to step inside and ease past him into the hallway of the house. There is stubble on his chin and creases in his white cotton shirt. I smell his breath and catch a hint of old sweat. He places a hand on my shoulder, digging his fingers in. "What the hell are you doing here, little brother?"

"It's freezing." I pull my donkey jacket tighter around me, words pluming in the chilled air. "Do you want to put the heating on?"

"What heating?" I follow him into the living room. "I've got an electric fire somewhere but I thought I'd save it until after Christmas. Keep the bills down. Anyway, you get used to it. It's not so bad."

"You're not even wearing a jumper."

"It's you who feels the cold, Nick. Always was." I put a hand on the pale emulsioned wall. It feels slick and damp. He sighs. "You may as well sit down, now you're here. I'll make some tea."

The faded gold Dralon settee sags as I lower myself onto it and the cushions are clammy to the touch. There's a pair of matching chairs opposite and a drop leaf table and a kitchen chair against one wall. There's a half-empty bottle of Bell's whisky on the table. A dark brown cord carpet covers the floor along with a circular, vaguely patterned rug.

I call through the half-open door into the kitchen. "How many rooms upstairs?"

I hear the kettle coming to the boil and the clink of teaspoons on china. "Just two. Bedroom and bathroom."

"You do have hot water, I suppose?"

"Of course," Patrick says, pushing the door fully open, two yellow mugs in one hand, a box of Jaffa cakes in the other. "I'm not an idiot."

I take my mug and warm my hands on it. Patrick settles in one of the chairs. "So?" he says, looking at me. I say nothing. When it comes to it, I don't know what to say. "Okay. How's Hannah?"

That gets a response, as he knows it will. "Don't."

He drinks some tea. His dark hair, which is receding slightly, is flecked with the first traces of grey. "Don't what?"

"Don't pretend to give a shit about Hannah."

I can't look at him and I'm pretty sure he's not looking at me. "I thought she might have sent you."

"Why the hell would Hannah send me?"

"Right." He puts his mug on the floor. There's colour in his cheeks. "Why *are* you here, then? Having a little gloat, are you?"

It's a good question. I don't know why I'm there. "Curious, that's all. Wanted to see where you've washed up. Thought you were a city boy. Never saw you ending up in a place like this."

"Couldn't stay with mum for ever. You'd know all about that, of course."

"But this is the arse end of nowhere. And this place ..."

"What about it?"

"It's a dump, Patrick. And it's freezing, I just don't…"

"Now who's pretending to care? So it's guilt, is it? That's why you're here? You know what you can do with your guilt, Nick."

"It's not guilt," I lied. "You're still my brother. I just wanted to see …"

"See what? You cheeky twat. Remind me who's living in my house again?"

"It's not your house, as you very well know." I'm not scared of him, not anymore, but I can still feel his anger building from metres away. "I thought we were past all that."

"Past it? We'll never be past it." He stands abruptly and grabs the bottle of whisky. He splashes some into his tea. He doesn't offer me any.

"I don't want to argue."

"I didn't ask you to come."

"No. You didn't."

"You took me by surprise." He sits again. He looks drained and old.

"I should have called ahead."

"Look, I've got work in a bit. I've got some shifts at a pub in King's Lynn."

"Okay. I'll make a move."

"Finish your tea first. And your biscuit."

"It's a cake."

"What?"

"They're called Jaffa Cakes. The clue's in the name."

"Piss off, Nick."

Ten minutes later I leave. At the car I turn, but Patrick has already shut the door behind him. I stand with my hands in my pockets and look at the house, the fields surrounding it, the beginnings of fenland and the marshes beyond them. Everywhere seems damp. I am sure that there is someone standing behind me but when I turn, the flat countryside is empty beyond eyesight.

"What were you expecting? A hug?" Hannah says. She's standing by the worktop in the kitchen, waiting for the kettle to boil.

"Hardly. It was just something I had to do, that's all."

"And that's that then, is it? We can draw a line now, can we? Put it behind us." She joins me at the kitchen table, tucking her knees in. "Put him behind us."

"The kettle's boiled."

"I know. I don't even want a drink. It's just habit, isn't it?"

I have the Mirror in front of me, open at the sports pages. I close it and fold it neatly in half.

"Were you looking at the racing pages?"

"As if," I say, smiling. I push the paper away from me.

"Seriously? I don't want to nag, but ..."

I make myself a coffee that I neither need nor want. With my back to her I say, "You're not nagging. I understand. But it's fine. It's all fine."

I hear the chair scrape as she stands. She comes to my side. She smells of peaches. "I wouldn't quite say that."

"What?"

"I forgot to tell you. Your mum called."

"Oh good," I say.

Neither of us can be bothered to cook so we order a Chinese takeaway. We eat in the living room. We drink wine, something chilled and dry and white. I'm not sure of the vintage or if it even has one. It's fine. It does the job.

We don't say much. I think about putting some music on but I don't quite get around to it. Later there's something we were going to watch together on TV but we don't get around to that either.

The evening passes, as they tend to do. Hannah stands and stretches. "I'm full and tired and just the tiniest bit drunk. I'm going to bed."

"Okay."

She comes across to me and ruffles my hair for no obvious reason. "Are you coming?"

She's neat and slender with an angled poise that often catches me unawares. "Not yet. I'll tidy up I think."

"It can wait."

"It's fine."

"You haven't called your mum."

"It's a bit late now. I'll do it tomorrow."

"I do believe that's called prevarication."

"I do believe that's correct."

She kisses me and smiles.

When she's gone I sit in the burgundy leather armchair and gaze at the congealing food on the coffee table. The living room is long and narrow with a pale honey-coloured carpet and off-white walls and a pine-panelled ceiling with spotlights inlaid. Hannah re-decorated after Patrick left. It's our house now; a semi-detached on the Thorpe Marriot estate, just outside Norwich, with two bedrooms and a small garden and a glut of memories. I tried to persuade her to move. *Why*, she said. *It was Patrick that hurt me, not the house. I want to stay.* I didn't argue. But then I rarely do.

I clear the food away and walk into the kitchen and rinse out our wine glasses. The heating has been off for a while and I shiver and think of Hannah in our warm bed. I pull the kitchen curtains together. Beyond them the night is still and cold. I think of Patrick in his freezing cottage, drinking tea.

I make my way upstairs eventually. Hannah is sleeping heavily and I don't wake her.

The next day is Sunday and my mother's phone call wakes me a little before 9.30. She doesn't say much, but I'm still left the usual guilt, the familiar conviction that I've done something wrong. I lie on my back and listen to the rain gusting against the bedroom window and to Hannah ratting around downstairs.

Chapter 2

Late in the morning Hannah and I wade through the leaf mulch and a cold drizzle and watch part of a football match at Sloughbottom Park. Hannah wears her long black coat and woollen hat and a burgundy scarf and she keeps a gloved hand clenched tightly in mine. Sometimes I regulate the strength of her grip, waiting for it to slacken. And I watch her face; her expression as she looks at me. Waiting for the cracks to show. It's just a matter of time.

But for now she leans against me as we watch a defender with a beer belly launch a clearance into a puddle near the far touchline.

We leave before the end of the match. My feet are numb with cold. The rain has stopped but the wind has an icy edge. The light is sour and acidic.

"So," Hannah says, as we pass a pair of wary, over-weight black Labradors. "What did mother dear have to say?"

"Not a lot. She wants to know what we're doing for Christmas. Thinks we should all get together." Hannah's silence is palpable. "I stalled her. We can go to your parents, can't we?"

"Not really. They're going to Australia for Christmas."

"Shit. Since when?"

"They told me a couple of weeks ago."

"Thanks for sharing."

"Slipped my mind."

"Australia. I thought Derek was a traditional Christmas kind of guy."

"So did I. Something they've always wanted to do, apparently. I'm a bit upset by it, to be honest. Don't tell mum, though."

"Can't we go with them?"

She laughs shortly. "I think not."

"Well, it's only November. Plenty of time to put mum off. You'll see."

Hannah says nothing.

At home we have hot showers and change our clothes and eat cheese on toast for lunch. We drink tea at the kitchen table. Hannah's hair is wet and falls partially across her face. She looks at me occasionally, her expression quizzical. We don't speak much. I pull the curtains early and switch the lamp on. We listen as the wind picks up and fresh rain hammers against the window.

I wonder what the weather is like in King's Lynn and I think of Patrick again. I look around the room he had once lived in and half expect him to step out of the shadows. Hannah dozes in the chair opposite, a paperback half-open in her hand. In the lamplight I think I can see the ghosts of old bruises on her cheeks.

We have a roast dinner later and Hannah chats a little about work and her sister's new boyfriend and I nod in the right places and grunt occasionally.

Afterwards in the kitchen as she washes and I wipe, she says, "It's a good sign, isn't it?"

"What?" I say.

"Comfortable silences. In a relationship." She wipes an already dry plate drier still. "It's good that we're easy in each other's company. Don't feel the need to run on all the time. About nothing." She shoots me a bright, empty grin. "That'd be sad, wouldn't it?"

"Desperately," I say.

"That's what I thought." She looks at the plate, frowns, and starts wiping it again.

Before we leave the kitchen she kisses me for no reason. Stands on her toes and puts her hands on my shoulders and leans against me. She tastes of the fruit salad we had for dessert.

"What was that for?"

"Because," she says.

There's some Dickens production on TV and we watch it together. I sit on the sofa. She lies across it with her feet on my lap. I listen to the rain and wonder if Monday's race meetings will have to be abandoned. I stroke Hannah's feet absently. I glance at her face from time to time, watching her expression, waiting for it to change.

Chapter 3

At seven-thirty the next morning I'm sitting in a plywood hut in the corner of a building site in a cul-de-sac off Unthank Road. Dan, my business partner, sits opposite, perched on top of a pile of pallets. He's dressed against the cold in a heavy sheepskin-lined bomber jacket over a sweater and a flannel shirt. He's short and heavily built. His hands are huge, gloveless, ingrained with brick dust. His face is grey in the half-light that struggles in through the dirty window.

He pours some strong coffee from a thermos flask into a dirty white plastic mug. "Where did you get too, then? Friday?"

"Friday?"

"Jesus, Nick." He seems tired, I think, rather than angry. Perhaps he is. He has every right to be both.

"I didn't think you'd be working, Dan. It was pissing down. Can't believe you were digging out footings in that."

"We didn't have much choice. As you know. The Readimix lorry's coming later. Can't put that off."

"You should have called."

"You should have turned your phone on."

"Yeah. Sorry, mate. What can I say?"

He stands and pulls the door open and tosses his coffee dregs onto the cold grass. "Nothing. As usual."

"Anyway, you don't need me. You've got the subbies. I'm crap at this stuff."

"I just needed a hand, Nick. That's all."

"Well, I'm here now."

"I've got enough on my plate as it is. Alice is teething, Beth is so knackered she doesn't know which way her arse is hanging. And it's all my fault, obviously, even though I was up at stupid o'clock this morning changing nappies." Dan is a quiet man for the most part, gently spoken and slow to anger, which is probably just as well from my point of view. This is quite a rant by his standards. His voice has risen an octave or two and he is pointing at me with the hand that holds the coffee cup.

"Finished?" His arm falls to his side. "I did warn you about having kids."

"Fuck off, Nick. What would you know about that?"

"Not a lot. Same as most things really." I smile in an attempt to break the tension. It fails, of course.

There's some surveying equipment in the corner of the hut. He passes me the staff and tripod. "Come on. Make yourself useful. The sooner we get these levels taken the sooner we can get these footings dug."

"I'm free until twelve."

"Twelve? Why twelve?"

"You know. Meetings. Money stuff. That's how it works, isn't it? My brains, your brawn. That's why we make such a good team."

"You're a cunt," he says quietly as he shoves the hut door open. I follow him out into the frigid air.

Dan and I have known each other for years. We were friends at school, of sorts, and kept loosely in touch ever since. Dan went into business with his dad and they handled extensions and small works all around the city until his dad died suddenly, on site, of a heart attack. At the funeral Dan told me that the business was on its last legs, his dad had no great business sense and what money there was had almost gone. So I helped him out, put some cash in, played at being a builder for a while. It's much more serious for Dan; it's his livelihood and he's continuing his father's work. And he's good at it, juggling half a dozen or so sites that we have on the go around the city; extensions, re-modelling, occasionally something from scratch. He keeps a small core of sub-contractors happy and busy, which is no small feat in itself. They like and trust him. They are much more wary around me, an outlook that I quite understand. I've just chucked some money in and turn up now and then in my shiny new work boots. If I was them I'd despise me.

But despite that and for all his growing resentment Dan knows that if I pull out he's in trouble. It turns out that as hard as he grafts he has about as much financial sense as his father. Actually so do I. I'm just much better at pretending otherwise.

So when lunchtime comes and I say I have to be off he grumbles a bit and calls me some names but I leave anyway and I don't look back.

The good thing about working on Unthank Road is that there's a Ladbrokes a five minute walk away. It's tucked down a side street which is even better as there is less chance of anyone I know seeing me go in or out.

I feel a familiar easing in my gut as I enter. It's easier these days to bet online, I suppose, but I'm old school, I prefer cash, over the counter, red plastic seats and an array of big screens. And this way, if I'm careful, there's less chance of Hannah finding out.

The place is almost empty, which is no great surprise on a dull Monday lunchtime with racing still an hour away. There is one other customer; a middle-aged bearded guy who feeds coins into a fixed odds machine by the far wall. I've seen him before but we don't acknowledge each other. This is no place for friendships or alliances.

Ray's behind the counter. He has greying hair cut very short and a brisk moustache. He wears his red Ladbrokes tie as louchely as possible. Which isn't saying much.

As I approach the counter he slaps a cardboard cup of anaemic-looking tea in front of me. "On the house," he says.

"Be still my beating heart."

"We do like to look after our premium customers."

"Noted," I say. "I'll tell all my friends."

"All of them? I'm not sure I could stand the rush." There's a little Irish in his accent sometimes. It comes and goes.

I sip the tea. "Jesus."

"Well, it's free, at least."

"How are things, Ray? It's been a while."

"I saw you Friday, Nick."

"Indeed. What can I say, it was a long weekend."

"You may tell me more if you wish." He raises his arms outward in an expansive gesture. "I've got little else to do."

"Kind of you," I say and mean it. "But it's okay. How was your weekend?"

"Outstanding."

"And the lovely Mrs Ray?"

"Transcendent."

"Great." I survey the empty shop. "Is there actually any racing on today?"

"Not a lot. Main meets washed out. We've got Southwell, of course. And a jumps meeting in Ireland. Clonmell."

Southwell. All weather dross; sellers, auction races, low grade handicaps. Slow horses and no-hopers. I'll still back them though. "Great."

"You don't have to actually have a bet, Nick."

I drink some tea. "Interesting concept."

The shop fills up a little as the afternoon wears on. The clientele, including myself, seem to match the horses on show; low grade, burnt out, scarcely visible at all.

I stay until just after four. I drink some more tea and a couple of cokes. I speak to no-one except Ray. I lose about fifty pounds over the course of the afternoon. I'm two hundred down at one point, but the last horse I back wins so I end on a high.

"Good times," I say as I cash in my final slip.

"Does Hannah know you're here?" Ray says.

I stuff the notes into my pocket.. "Every time you ask me that and every time I don't answer."

He pushes a smile of sorts past his moustache. "I suppose it's just that thing we do, isn't it?"

"I suppose it is," I say.

Chapter 4

It's Wednesday afternoon and I'm sat on an orange beanbag in the living room of a shabby house off Brunswick Road. Tash sits opposite me. Her beanbag is purple with mint-green piping. A Calor gas heater squats in the middle of the room, all three bars on. There are no other chairs, just a table of sorts. The flat reminds me of Patrick's cottage. Except it's warmer.

Tash lies back with her eyes closed, smoking a joint. Her jeans are torn and paint-stained. She wears a shapeless rust-coloured sweater. Her hair is dyed red and has no discernible style.

"Racing off, is it?" she says. She blows smoke lazily towards the ceiling.

"No."

"I'm honoured then."

"I suppose."

"I nearly didn't let you in. it's a bit presumptuous. I could have been otherwise engaged."

"I expect you'd have let me know."

"I expect I would."

"The thing is, I keep losing."

She opens an eye. "Am I your therapist?"

"It's an occupational hazard, I agree. A side effect. If one gambles, one may lose. But … there are limits."

She closes her eye again and lets her head fall back. "Okay."

"Some people say that gambling addicts want to lose. As a way of punishing themselves."

"That's deep."

"I don't want to lose. I like winning. It's nice. It's not really about the money though."

"Whatever you say, Nick."

"But I'm not sure that Hannah would see it that way."

She sits up. "Does Hannah know? Is that what all this is about?"

"No. I don't think so."

She stubs out her joint. "She will, though. One day. You know that, don't you?"

"I suppose that I do."

Tash works behind the bar of the *Oak*, a nondescript pub a ten minute walk away from her flat. We met there one chilly afternoon the previous winter.

I was going through one of my regular, if brief, periods of abstinence as far as gambling was concerned, but I couldn't face work or Dan so I ducked into the *Oak* on an impulse and ordered a lager and a whisky and a packet of cheese and onion crisps.

"Sophisticated," the girl behind the bar said.

"That's me. It's a bit dead in here, isn't it?" It was something of an understatement. The curtains were pulled across and the bar was dark and still and heavy with the scent of old beer. I was the only customer.

"Three o'clock on a Tuesday afternoon? What do you expect?" Her hair was longer then and coloured with hints of green, not red.

She served me and I paid her. "I asked for cheese and onion crisps." I dangled the bag of salt and vinegar she'd given me in front of her.

"Did you?" She shrugged and made no attempt to

correct her error. I laughed and she said, "First world problems, mate."

We chatted because there was nothing else to do. She was a student, she said. Off and on. Had been for a while, by the sounds of it and it was effort making ends meet but it was worth it as the alternative was going back to her parents in Swindon. They didn't like her living here, she said, didn't want her to be independent. But then she didn't like them much, so that was fair enough, she supposed. In the scheme of things.

"When do you graduate?"

"Graduate?" She pulled at a strand of hair and it wound around her finger. "Dunno. It's flexible, isn't it? Got to try different things, different courses, see what fits."

"Okay," I said.

There must have been something in my tone because she gave me a look and slammed the fresh pint I'd just ordered down in front of me so that beer slopped onto the counter. "Alright, smartarse. What do you do?"

"I'm a builder."

"You don't look like a builder."

She had a point. "I suppose I'm more of an entrepreneur."

"You don't look much like one of those either."

"This is no way to treat your only customer," I said, and I thought of Ray, suddenly, and how often I'd said the same thing to him.

"You can piss off if you want. Makes no difference to me." There was a little smile as she spoke though.

I stayed a bit longer, had a couple more drinks and bought her a couple too. There was a jukebox in the corner so I put on some MGMT and Bloc Party.

"Jesus. How are old are you?" I told her. "Well, you're younger than my dad, at least."

"That makes me feel all warm inside."

When the music and drink were finished I said, "I'd better be off."

She leant forward and braced her arms against the bar and looked right into my face. "I'm free in an hour. And my house is only a few minutes away."

I could smell the gin on her breath. "Okay."

"It'll cost you, of course."

"Cost me?"

"Not too much. Not really. But yeah." Her eyes didn't leave mine.

"Okay," I said.

"Are we going upstairs then?" Tash says after a while.

"If you like," I say.

"It's no skin off my nose."

I'm not sure I can be bothered. "I haven't got any cash on me."

"Stick it on the tab. I trust you. Kind of."

"Really?"

Her eyes widen. "I said, kind of. Jesus." She gathers herself and pulls at a strand of hair. "We may as well. You're here now."

I struggle out of the bean bag and onto my feet. It takes a while. "Come on then," I say.

It's cold in her bedroom but we warm each other up. Afterwards we huddle under a quilt that is the colour of custard and shiny with age. I have an arm around her as the bed is too small to lay together otherwise. She has a spray of freckles across the top of her shoulders and above her top lip and the bridge of her nose.

"Mum and dad are on at me again. About going home."

"Are you tempted?"

"Yes. No. I don't know."

"Decisive."

"I don't suppose this is ... sustainable. But ... Swindon, my folks? I'm not sure I can face it."

"How's Uni?"

"How do you think?"

"I really don't know, Tash. That's why I asked."

"I've skipped so many lectures, taken so many breaks. I don't even know what my fucking course is anymore."

"I'm sorry."

She turns towards me and I feel her breath on my face. "Sorry?"

I feel her small breast against my arm. "I don't know what else to say."

Her voice softens. "You don't have to say anything. I'm just talking, that's all."

"That's why I came here today. To talk. Not this. Nice as it was."

"We do talk. Well, you do. Afterwards. About Hannah mostly. But still. Perhaps I should charge extra."

"I mean ... just talk. Not this."

"Okay."

"I don't always have to come here. We could go for a coffee or something."

She's quiet for a while and I listen to her breathing. Then she says, "Jesus, Nick, how fucking lonely are you?"

As I'm dressing she says, "You know she'll find out? Hannah? About us. About whoever else you're screwing. About the gambling."

"It's a fair bet. Eventually."

"Don't you care?"

She's still naked on the bed, the quilt pulled under her chin. I button my shirt. "Of course I care."

"I thought you were her hero. Her knight in shining armour."

I stop buttoning. "I said that?"

"Kind of."

"I probably shouldn't have."

"Feet of clay," she says.

I finish dressing. "I've got to go."

I leave some notes on the dressing table.

"I thought you didn't have any cash?"

"I lied," I say.

Hannah has a PTA meeting so when I get home I have time to shower and change. I check the racing results and think that a couple of winners look like horses I might have backed but immediately dismiss the thought as an addict's self-deception. I check my overdraft on my phone and the state of the several credit cards I'm juggling and really wished that I hadn't.

"Good day?" Hannah's perfume billows over me as she bustles in, kissing my cheek and throwing her coat over the back of a chair.

"The usual," I say. "How was your meeting?"

"Oh, you know. Bloody parents, bloody kids. School would be fine if it wasn't for them. And the teachers, of course." I look at her flushed cheeks and bright eyes. "It wasn't too bad, actually." She wrinkles her nose. "I can't smell food, Nick."

"Shit. I was meant to cook, wasn't I? Sorry. I'll order a takeaway."

"No worries," Hannah says. "I'm not that hungry. I'll make a sandwich. Want one?"

I follow her into the kitchen. "Have you been drinking?"

She pulls some ham and cheese from the fridge. "A single gin and tonic. Why?" She toys with the mayo for a moment then leaves it where it is.

"Just wondered. You seem very mellow."

"Are you complaining?"

"Not at all."

"Good." She grins briefly, emptily. "Mustard or pickle?"

In the living room we eat sandwiches and drink beer. We turn the TV on briefly and let Bake Off play in the background. I watch Hannah lick a trace of mustard from her lips and I think of Tash and how her mouth tastes. I nearly tell Hannah then: about Tash, about the gambling and the steepling, vertiginous debts. I think perhaps that if I start to confess I will never stop. I imagine the expression on Hannah's face as I tell her. I say nothing.

Hannah goes to bed before me as usual. She kisses my cheek. Her lips are cold. I drink my beer slowly although I barely taste it at all. I can change, I think. I've been two days without a bet. I can give Tash up, I'm sure of that. The debts can be managed. I can even try working for a living. All things are possible, I think. I go to bed believing it.

Chapter 5

Hannah has already left for work when I wake. It's still dark and I hear the wind outside. I pull the covers up to my chin for a moment then shrug them off. Under a long, hot shower I try to wash away the night's predictable dreams. They were of Tash mostly. At one point I woke, sweating and disorientated, convinced that I reeked of her, certain that at any moment Hannah would also wake and demand to know what the hell is going on.

I dress and drive to the extension we're building on Sprowston Road. Vic, one of our brickie's, is there on his own.

"Jesus," he says when he sees me. "To what do I owe the honour?" I stumble as I pick my way across the site towards him. "Careful, Nick. Probably not used to the terrain. This is a building site. These are bricks."

"It's nice to see that you're still such a sarky bastard, Vic." He laughs at that, but then he's pretty good natured for a man who rarely seems to see the good in anybody. Good brickie though. "Dan around?"

He pours himself some tea from a battered flask. He's about my height, broad-shouldered, with fair, thinning hair that is unevenly distributed. He has a vague agricultural air and his cheeks are as ruddy as a pig farmer's. "Trying to find out where my labourer has got to. I can't get hold of him and he should have been here ages ago."

"Can't get the staff."

Vic grunts and sips some tea. "You can knock us up a mixer load of mortar, if you like? This lots nearly done."

"Love to. Can't. Places to be. You know how it is."

"Right. Family okay?" I nod. "How's that brother of yours? You see much of him these days?"

His expression is guileless. "Not much. When you see Tim tell him I dropped in?"

"Course. Red letter day." He screws the lid back on his flask. "He's after you actually. Some supplier playing silly buggers. Account's overdue, they reckon."

"Computer playing up, I expect."

"I expect." He turns the handle on the cement mixer and it starts on the second pull.

"See you, then," I say.

Vic shovels sand and keeps his head down and doesn't answer.

My car is parked on the road and I sit in it and listen to the grind and churn of the mixer. It's barely ten-thirty. I could stay with Vic and put in a couple of hours of physical work. That was my intention. I'd come dressed for it. I drive away from Sprowston Road without looking back.

"This is a surprise," my mother says, fumbling the chain from the door and pushing it all the way open. I take off my coat and follow her down the familiar hallway. She still lives in the same semi-detached on Dereham Road that Patrick and I had been brought up in. I feel no sense of the past here, though. No weight of memories. I feel nothing at all. "Is it Patrick? Is he ill? I told him, living in that freezing ..."

"Don't panic. I'm at a loose end, that's all." In the living room I fold my coat across the back of a chair in which my father had once sat.

"You'll want tea, I suppose? And biscuits?" My mother has shrunk over the years but she is still nimble enough with bright blue eyes that miss nothing. She wears a green-checked housecoat and her usual expression; slightly sour, an eyebrow half-raised, that air of faint accusation.

"Don't put yourself out." I follow her into the kitchen. Like the rest of the house it is spotlessly clean. And, like the rest of the house, it is soulless, devoid of warmth. And there is an air of faint dilapidation. Nothing you can pin down. Individual things – the sink, the worktop – are clean, neat, tidy, but there is a cumulative sense of shabbiness that no amount of pine-scented cleaner can cover up. Or perhaps that is simply the memories that I deny; a whole clutter of them, crammed into corners, gathering dust. I take a breath. "Actually, it's about Christmas. We can't make it. Sorry."

She's at the sink, fiddling with the kettle. "Why ever not?"

I look out of the window at the small shingled drive. "We're going away. Don't know where yet. It's going to be a last minute thing."

"That's strange. Hannah didn't mention it."

"When did you speak to Hannah?" I don't try and keep the sharpness out of my voice.

"Yesterday? Day before? We had quite a long chat. She didn't say anything about you going away."

I stare at her, but she busies herself with the kettle. "You had a long chat? With Hannah?"

"Is that so unusual?"

"Yes. It is. You've hardly had a civil word for her since Patrick left."

She pauses a moment, steadying herself. "Perhaps I was a little hard on her."

"Fucking hell. Have you had a blow to the head or something?"

"Nicholas. Language." Thin sunlight spears through the window and falls into the lines on her face and neck. "Anyway. You're avoiding the subject."

I find the biscuit tin and rummage at the bottom until I locate a custard cream. "It was going to be a surprise."

"A surprise." Her expression is mild, her eyes soft now, and unfocused. "I'm an old woman. I don't expect I've got many Christmas's left. Can't you humour me?"

"You can't expect Hannah to eat Christmas dinner with Patrick."

"Who said anything about Patrick? I haven't heard from him for weeks. I expect he's got his own plans."

I watch her for a moment. "Are you serious? No Patrick at Christmas? And you're being civil to Hannah? I assume that's the apocalypse I hear thundering towards us."

"You're not funny, Nicholas. You always think you are funny. But you're not."

I almost laugh.

We drink our tea in the living room. I sit on a sofa that is years old and has been re-covered at least a half-dozen times. The teapot and our cups stand on a pine coffee table that my father made thirty years ago. We're silent for several minutes. My tea is hot and I have to drink it slowly. Small talk is not one of mother's strengths. At least not with me. Eventually I say, "I must be off. Things to do."

"Nice of you to drop in." Her voice is without

inflection, her face flat. We both stand. "You're seeing someone, aren't you?"

"What?"

"Guilt. You stink of it." She smiles and her head tips to one side. "And you're gambling again."

"No."

"I can read you like a book."

"You're just guessing."

"Can't look at me though, can you?" She passes me my coat and I snatch it off her. "You should never have left that job."

"They made me redundant. How many times?"

"But why you? Do you ever wonder that?"

Her eyes are narrow, her shoulders set. I say nothing and make my way to the door. She follows me. "I'll be in touch about Christmas. Sort out the details."

I slam the door shut without looking back.

"Are you going to sulk all evening?" Hannah says. She's on the sofa with her legs crossed, the evening paper folded in her lap.

"I'm not sulking. I'm pissed off." I'm trying to read a paperback but I can't get to the end of the page.

"Okay."

I mark my place in the book and toss it onto the table. "And you were late again."

I expect her to snap then. She's indulged my childishness since I confronted her with my mother's revelations a couple of hours earlier. Instead she picks up her wineglass, looks at it, puts it down again. "It was just a quick drink. I've told you about Sarah? She's got man problems. Wanted a chat."

"Okay. But you know we'll be spending Christmas at my mother's now, don't you?"

"Perhaps it won't be so bad."

"What?"

"Look, I've said I'm sorry. I should have told you I was talking to your mum, but I knew you'd be like this. I thought I was building bridges. I think she's really making an effort."

"Did she mention Patrick?"

"Not really."

"Not really?"

She reaches for the wineglass and this time she drinks from it. Her hair is wet from the shower. She wears a lemon-coloured dressing gown and pink slippers. "She said he always had a temper. She said she was sorry. Sorry for everything."

"Sorry? My mother said she was sorry?" Hannah nods. "Fuck me," I say.

We drink some more wine and I thaw a little. I keep looking at the colour in her cheeks and the brightness of her eyes. I touch her arm. "Fancy an early night?"

"That's subtle. You could hardly bring yourself to talk to me earlier."

"I'm sorry. I'm an idiot sometimes."

She smiles oddly and touches my face. "I can't anyway. Time of the month."

"Of course," I say. "No problem."

A little later I go to bed and I'm asleep before she comes up.

Chapter 6

On Saturday evening Hannah and I meet Jessica and her boyfriend Jake at the Thai restaurant in St Gregory's Alley. Jessica is younger than her sister. She has amber coloured eyes and fair, slightly reddish hair cut short. Both sisters wear short black dresses, a little jewellery, a minimal amount of make-up. Both look stunning. Jake is younger than me, taller, rake thin. He wears a jacket that is too big for him and a tie fastened in a loose knot. He has a small, untidy beard and nervous eyes. He exudes the air of someone who is trying too hard.

The restaurant has a low ceiling and the lighting is muted. The food is suitably spicy, in fact my chilli beef is too hot and I can't finish it.

"Wimp," Hannah says. She takes a mouthful. Her face is expressionless for a moment then her eyes water. "Bloody hell." She drinks some wine.

"Told you." My mouth still burns.

Jessica and Jake sit opposite us. Jessica's eyes seem a different shade of amber depending on her mood. Now they are deep and rich, almost coffee coloured. Jake has long slender fingers that keep pulling at the tablecloth, his tie, his beard. He chats erratically during the meal. There are local elections coming up and he keeps touching on that. I don't much like what he has to say, but I feel Hannah nudge me as I start to respond so I keep my mouth shut.

"We've got an announcement," Jessica says as they clear our plates away. Her face shines. Jake looks at the wall.

"Oh God, you're not pregnant, are you?" Hannah says.

"What? No." She smiles and thrusts her hands onto the table. "Jake and I are going to live together."

"It's a bit sudden, isn't it?" Hannah says.

"No," Jessica says quickly. "When you know, you know. I've never met anyone like Jake."

"I'll bet," I say.

"What?" Jake says.

"Nothing." I feel Jake's eyes on me. I look at Jessica. "I wish you well."

She rewards me with a sweet smile. "Jake's moving into mine. My place is bigger and, well, nicer, frankly."

I bite my lip.

"Have you told Mum and Dad?" Hannah says.

"I thought Jake could move in while they're away. I'll tell them when they get back."

Hannah snorts, "Yeah, that'll work."

"It will actually. Fait accompli, as they say. Telling them might be a bit grim, though."

"Just a bit."

"How about you, Jake? How do you feel?" I say.

"Jessica means everything to me. And she keeps me rooted, you know? Focused."

"Focused? You're a student, aren't you? How focused do you need to be?"

"Nick," Hannah says.

"And I'm joining the Green Party," Jessica says, squeezing Jake's hand.

"That's nice," Hannah says. "Just don't go off whaling, will you?"

"Whaling?" We all look at her.

She frowns. "I mean trying to stop the whaling. In those little boats."

"That's Greenpeace," I say.

"Oh," Hannah says.

Later we go for a drink at the *Ten Bells*. Jessica's choice. It's small and eclectic and oddly set out. Something gritty and downbeat plays on the jukebox. Hannah and Jake find a table while Jessica and I fight our way to the bar.

"You don't like him, do you?" Jessica says. A tall man with dyed black hair squeezes past us.

"Nothing to do with me."

"It's written all over your face."

"Well. He's too young for you. And he's a fucking Tory."

"He literally just told you he's a Green."

"No point voting Green here."

"That doesn't make him a Tory."

"If you don't vote Labour in Norwich you may as well be a Tory."

"He's got convictions. That's more than can be said for you."

I shrug. A young woman wearing a velvet choker and too much make-up smiles at me and I smile back.

Jessica's expression changes. "You're jealous, aren't you?" We'd had a fling once. A brief one, years before, when Hannah was with Patrick.

"Dream on."

"I've seen you looking at me."

"I still care about you. You're Hannah's sister, after all."

Her face goes wistful. "Hannah," she says. "It's her you should be worried about."

"Meaning?"

She looks into my face and starts to speak and then the barman is there, hands on the bar, leaning towards her.

"Yes, love?" he says. His hair is fair and thick and matted with sweat.

Jessica orders. I let her pay. As we sort our drinks out she says, "God, I'm dying for a fag."

"Well, you're a big girl. Have one."

"And let Hannah know I smoke? She'd do her nut. And she'd tell Mum and Dad."

"Hannah's no grass."

"Right," Jessica says. "Good old Hannah. Butter wouldn't melt."

I follow her back to the table. The black dress is tight across her thighs and hips.

Afterwards we walk to the Guildhall to find a taxi. The air is cold and still. As Hannah and Jessica hug and say their goodbyes Jake takes me to one side. "I think you've got some issues, man."

"Indeed I have. So many issues. Man."

"It's clear you don't like me. I don't hold it against you."

"Thank goodness for that."

He gives me a look, starts to say something, changes his mind. Then Jessica ushers him over to the taxi. "Are you sure you don't want to share?" Hannah says to me. I shake my head. We wave as they drive off. We stand on the pavement.

"We'll catch one in a minute," I say.

"Could have shared."

"I don't like him, Hannah."

"So I'd gathered. I think he's nice."

"Each to their own."

"Mum and Dad will go ballistic, though."

"Naturally."

She hunches her shoulders against the cold, moves close to me and leans her head on my chest, which surprises me. I put my arms around her. A taxi comes and takes us home. We go to bed and make love for the first time in six weeks. That surprises me as well.

Chapter 7

The next Thursday I'm at home with a cold when Dan comes to the door. He takes his working boots off and enters the living room. "Coffee?" I say.

"I haven't got time. I'm at Sprowston Road on my own."

"Sorry." I cough a couple of times. "I'd help if I could. Feel like shit though."

"Don't worry about it."

"Sit down, at least."

He shakes his head. "Nick, I need to know. Is everything okay? The business, I mean. Money. Cash flow. Whatever the fuck you want to call it."

I try to look indignant. "What sort of question is that? Vic said something about suppliers playing up. Is that it? It's all sorted. Give me some credit, will you?"

"I'd rather know, that's all. If it's all going tits up … I'd rather know. I've worked too hard …"

I put my hand on his arm. "I know. I know you have. You get paid, though, don't you? The subbies get paid. It's all fine."

"Your phone is never on, Nick."

"I don't really like them, mate. I'm a bit old school. Look, I'll get dressed, come and give you a hand."

He stares at me for a moment then shakes his head. "No. You look terrible. You stay here. I'll be okay. As long as the other stuff is okay, I'll be okay."

"You have my word."

He looks into my face for a moment then pats my arm and leaves. I watch him drive away. I stand at the window for a long time, gazing out at the empty street.

The next day I feel a little better and I drive into the city centre. I mooch around Waterstone's and flick through the CD's in HMV. Old school indeed. At lunchtime I have a toasted cheese and ham sandwich and a latte in Costa. I sit in a window seat and sip my coffee and watch the shoppers trudge past Primark and FatFace. There's a builder's skip outside Primark and almost everyone who passes it glances briefly at its contents. The day is dull and mild and blustery.

I push my empty plate to one side and concentrate on the coffee. It seems odd, feeling so calm. I work out how many days it has been since my last bet. Then I try to convert it into hours, minutes, seconds, but I can't do it. I try and fail to remember the name of the last horse that I'd bet on. I wonder what trainers are in form now, what jockeys. I find that I don't care. I think that it's a good sign. I try to pretend that the gnawing in the pit of my stomach is an illusion, something I can easily control.

Then I try to work out how much money I owe, how close the company is to folding. My mind keeps veering away from the figures. It simply won't let them form. I drink some coffee.

I think of Hannah. And Jessica. And Tash. And as I think of her, there she is. Tash. A dozen yards away, beyond the window, wearing a navy anorak that is a couple of sizes too big, walking in the direction of Marks and Spencer. Beside her is a tall man wearing a dark grey woollen overcoat with the collar up. His long black hair is tied back in a ponytail. They are hand in hand. He glances towards her and it looks as though he says something. She turns and looks up into his face. She smiles.

"I just want to know his name," I say. "Is that so unreasonable?"

"Well, yes, actually." Tash is staring at me, her eyes wide open. "On account of it being none of your fucking business."

"You don't have to shout."

"Well, what the fuck have you been doing?"

Tash's housemate, Kirsty, stands in the corner. She is short and plump with an anxious, moon-shaped face and straight sandy hair. She's been very quiet but now she says, "Do you want me to call the police, Tash?"

"That's not such a good idea, is it, Kirsty?" Tash says, slowly, patiently. "Think about it."

Enlightenment shades Kirsty's features. "Still, it's not right, is it? Him just barging in and shouting and stuff."

"It's okay," Tash says. "Just go to your room for a bit. Nick will be leaving soon, won't you, Nick?"

I say nothing. Kirsty leaves and Tash and I are alone in their bleak, bare living room.

She sits on a beanbag, hugging her knees. I stand. She wears a toffee-coloured sweater and a short skirt with navy woollen tights and black DM's. "Do you think I sit here and wait for you?"

"No. I don't know. No. Of course not."

"You pay me, Nick." She says the words very quietly and slowly, as though she's speaking to a child.

After a moment I say, "Does he pay you?"

"Fuck off."

"And there are others, I assume? Do they all pay you?"

She stands, her body rigid. "Seriously, Nick. Fuck off. I don't care about the dope. I'll call the police."

"I'm sorry."

"You should leave."

"I'm really sorry, Tash."

She takes a long shuddering breath. "You fucking should be."

"I don't know what's wrong with me."

"You've never cared. You're always such a sarcastic prick. I kinda like that about you."

"It's one of my best features."

She almost smiles. "His name's Cameron. I met him at the bar. It's not serious. Not yet."

"Have you slept with him?"

"I can't believe that you asked me that."

"And yet, I did."

She sighs. "No. I haven't. Not yet."

"Right."

"Jesus. And I suppose you and Hannah are in separate beds?"

"Might as well be."

"Oh, come on."

"Seriously. And there isn't anybody else."

"What are you saying?"

"I don't know."

She reaches for the tobacco tin then leaves it where it is. "I like things how they are."

"Well, you would. What with the money and all."

I hope that my smile will take the edge off my words and it seems that they do. "It was never about the money."

"Okay."

"I was taking the piss. I couldn't believe you fell for it. And then you paid me and I thought ... why not."

"Why not indeed."

"I mean, you're pretty old but you're fit enough. All things considered."

"Thanks."

"And we talk sometimes. Don't we?"

"We do."

"We talk shit, for the most part. But I like it. Kind of."

"So do I, as it happens."

"So what the fuck are we doing?"

"I don't know."

"Are you still gambling?"

"Not for a while."

She nods. She picks up the tobacco tin again and runs it around and around in her fingers. "That's good." She leans back against the wall. Her eyes are very wide and her mouth is small and soft.

"I suppose I should go."

"I suppose you should." I don't move. "We could go upstairs though. If you want."

"We could," I say.

And we do.

A little later, as we are getting our breath back, there's a knock on the door. A voice says, "You okay in there, Tash?"

"Everything's fine, Kirsty," Tash says. Then, in a quieter voice. "She loves the drama, that one." She lies back. I put my hand on her stomach. "Something's changed," she says.

"Yes."

She turns towards me, slides an arm around my chest. "You know what I mean? Something's different between us."

"Yes," I say. "Something's different."

*

I'm home before Hannah again. I've showered and changed and am cooking pasta when she comes in. "Nick, I'm sorry."

"It's okay. Sarah?"

"Sarah? Yes. I lost track of time. That smells nice. You are a sweetheart."

We eat in an odd, charged silence. There are lines under Hannah's eyes and her cheeks seem hollow and pinched. I almost say something then; about Tash. I keep bracing myself for it but somehow the silence stretches on. "You okay?" I say eventually.

She puts her fork on the table and looks up. "No. My head is throbbing. I'm sorry. I come in late and I'm being such a moody cow."

"Don't be silly."

"I'm going to bed. Is that okay?"

"You don't need to ask. Perhaps you should call in sick tomorrow?"

"I'll be fine after a night's sleep." She kisses my cheek and makes her way to the stairs.

I listen to her climb them. I hear her in the bathroom and then the creak of the bed. I stare at my empty plate for a while before I stand and take the dinner things into the kitchen.

Chapter 8

On Saturday Hannah decides to visit her sister. "It's been a while," she says. "And when Jake moves in things will change."

"You don't even like your sister."

We're in the kitchen. Hannah looks pale and beautiful. "I thought I'd stay at Jessica's tonight."

"And, to be frank, she doesn't like you."

"What?" Her eyes are out of focus and she appears distant, insubstantial.

"Nothing. Do you want me to come?"

"You'd be bored. Anyway, I expect Jake will be around. I know what you think of him." She smiles without quite looking at me.

"Okay. I've got plenty to do," I lie. "Are you sure you'll be okay driving? You still don't look well."

"It's Diss. I think I can manage."

"Still ..."

"Don't fuss, Nick." I look up at her. "Sorry, I didn't mean to snap." I gaze into my coffee. It sums up the week somehow. We are constantly on edge, always just out of synch. She sits at the table, rests her elbows on it. "I spoke to your mum again yesterday."

"Right."

"Sorting Christmas out. Times and stuff. It's not far off."

"Don't remind me."

"I'm looking forward to it." She appears to be serious. "She's going to do your favourites; honey roast parsnips."

"My favourites?"

"You should have said. We can do them anytime. No big deal."

"I don't remember them being my favourite."

"You loved them, she said. She ran on a bit about your old family Christmas's. Sounded quite wistful. Which isn't a word I'd usually associate with your mother."

"I don't remember them either."

"Really?"

"I'm sure that they happened. Not that I'd trust my mother's version. I just don't really remember. You don't talk about yours much, come to think of it?"

She shrugs. "Pretty standard. We were spoiled, I suppose. We took it for granted, Jessica and I. Still do, I reckon."

"You're not alone there."

"But I do have memories, Nick. The usual stuff; Dad carving the turkey, party hats, having to be quiet for the Queen's speech. And I remember pulling Jessica's hair when she got the doll that I wanted. I'm not proud of it, but it's there." She presses a finger against the side of her head. "But you and ..." Her voice falters.

"What?"

"Patrick. You and Patrick." It jars, her saying his name. It's as though she's smashed a glass on the kitchen floor. "He was the same. If I asked about the past." She mimics his voice. "I dunno. Don't remember. We'll talk about it later."

I think about her and her lack of openness about her own past, but I say nothing, as I always do. "Well ... our Dad died."

"I know and that's awful. But it's as though he never existed. Neither of you mention him, I haven't seen a single photo ..."

"We weren't big on family snaps."

"Ok. But still."

"Still, what?"

"It's not ..." She flounders briefly and I let her. "It's like you're blocking it all out."

After a moment I say, "Perhaps I am. Does it matter?"

"I think that it probably does, Nick." She speaks slowly and I catch a hint of the teacher in her; some concern, a little warmth, but mostly the sense of being very faintly patronised.

"I expect you're right, Hannah. You usually are."

Her body language changes and the tiny spots of colour that have formed high on her cheeks fade as quickly as they came. "It doesn't matter. I don't suppose it's really any of my business."

I could contradict her, but I don't.

A little later I help her carry her bags out to her Clio. I ask her to give Jessica my love and she says she will.

Inside I heat some soup and listen to Radio Five. I read the paper listlessly, avoiding the racing pages. There's a meeting from Ascot on the TV later. I eat half a bowl of soup and a bread roll. I go for a walk. The sun is low and the light is rich and buttery, the air too warm for early December.

Later I drive into the city, heading for Brunswick Road. I drive past Tash's house twice. I park on Newmarket Road and check my phone. Tash has left seven messages. I delete them and drive home.

I do some paperwork. Dan and I are owed some

money by tardy payers and think I can make myself useful for once by chasing them down. As I flick through the invoices I notice the time. The first race at Ascot is imminent. It can't hurt to watch it, I think. I'm just about to switch on the TV when the doorbell rings. I think it might be Tash so I open the door reluctantly.

"Hello, little brother," Patrick says.

I fetch him a beer and we sit in the living room. He's lost weight. He hasn't shaved for a while either and there are grey patches in his stubble. He wears his old leather jacket with an Arran sweater and worn jeans that look too big on him.

"Taking a risk, aren't you?" I say. "Just as well that Hannah's not here."

"I've got eyes. Her car's gone."

"You could have just called."

He takes a mouthful of beer, drinking from the bottle. "Where's the fun in that?"

I want him to go. I want to watch the racing. It isn't that I want a bet. At least, I don't think I do. "Have you called mum?"

He drains his beer in two more large swallows. "Have you got any more?" When I return with another bottle he's prowling around the living room. He stops to examine our modest collection of paperbacks. "I like what you've done with the place."

"It's all Hannah."

"Of course it is. But this is my house really. You know it. Hannah knows it." His voice is low and mild.

An enormous wave of tiredness washes over me. "Except it isn't. It really isn't. We've been through this. Look… I know it's …"

He snatches the bottle from my hand and points it towards me. "Don't …" I sense him trying to gather himself, attempting to dredge something from beyond the baggy sweater and the sallow skin. He fails. His arm drops. "Thanks for the beer."

"*Have* you spoken to Mum?"

He sits in Hannah's chair and crosses his legs. "I need some money."

"What?"

"I've been ill. Missed some work. No work, no pay. It'll be no house soon if I don't pay the rent."

"What's wrong with you?"

"Nothing much."

"I don't believe that." Patrick is famously physically robust. He's always considered this a sign of his moral superiority.

"Aches and pains. Joys of getting old."

"You're barely forty."

"Stop changing the subject."

It makes me uncomfortable seeing him in Hannah's chair. But not as uncomfortable as him asking me for money. "It's a bad time."

"What?"

"It's cash flow. We're owed loads. Give me a week or two and I'll see what I can do."

"Don't put yourself out." He coughs briefly and violently until his face turns the colour of brick. When he's finished he looks at me as though nothing has happened.

"Do you want some water?"

"Are you afraid of upsetting Hannah?"

"It's not that," I say, surprising myself by realising that it's true.

"You're gambling again." It isn't a question. He tries to keep his gaze on me, but neither of us are good with eye contact and his eyes cut away before I can answer.

"I'm not gambling. Not that it's any of your

ANDREW HUMPHREY

business." I stand and fish my wallet from my back pocket. I hand him two twenty pound notes.

He looks at them. "What good do you think they'll do?" I start to put them away but he snatches them from my hand. "One other thing," he says.

"What?"

"I've missed my bus. I'm going to need a lift home."

"I was going to watch the rugby," I say. We're on the A47, just past Easton. The sun is low and awkward and I keep squinting against it.

"Put the radio on."

"It's not the same." I glance at him. He looks wretched. "So how's it going? Living in the arse end of nowhere?"

"It's fine."

"And work?"

"As if you care."

"I'm asking, aren't I?"

He exhales loudly. "The hours are shit and so is the pay. Other than that it's great."

We're quiet for a while. Even with the windows wound up I can smell the fertiliser on the bare fields.

"I met a friend of yours, though. The other day. At the club."

"Club?"

"Where I work."

"I thought it was a pub."

"No. It's a club. Does it matter?" I shake my head. "It's called Hector's House. Do you know it?"

"I don't know King's Lynn. Who's the friend?"

"Richard Butler. You worked with him. And you used to hang about with him at school, didn't you?"

"Yeah."

I catch his smile out of the corner of my eye. "He was very chatty, was Richard. He was three sheets to the wind, mind you. Not a fan, of yours, though, Nick. Not a fan at all."

I shift uncomfortably. "Just say it, why don't you? You clearly can't wait."

"But there's no need, is there, little brother? You know. You were there, after all."

"I don't know what you're talking about."

"He was a bit hazy, with the drink on him. Embezzlement, was it? Something like that?"

"I wouldn't take too much notice of Richard. He's no angel. It's not as cut and dried as he'd have you think."

"Things rarely are. But … he was an old friend and he gave you a job and you screwed him over. That's the gist, isn't it?" I say nothing. "So all that stuff about redundancy? That was just to shut Mum up, was it?"

"What do you think?"

"Does Hannah know?" I click the radio on and say nothing. Perhaps he sees something in my face because the sneer goes out of his voice. "I won't say anything. Not to Mum, not to Hannah." I turn the radio up. England have just scored a try but miss the conversion. "I'm just winding you up, that's all." Then, after a moment, "When did you start gambling again?"

"I'm not gambling. Are you still drinking too much? It looks as though you are."

He shrugs and sighs. We pass the turning to Mattishall and the road curves to the left. The sky is vast and clear and empty.

*

I drop him at the door of his cottage. He doesn't ask me in. I'm struck again by the sense of isolation, by the bleak, angled sparseness of the countryside. The sky is larger still and emptier than ever. I stare at it hard and it stares right back. Norfolk skies never blink.

I watch Patrick walk to the door, his shoulders slumped. He looks old and defeated. I feel something twist inside me. He closes the door without a backward glance.

It's almost dark when I get back to Norwich. The sky is salmon-coloured, marbled with streaks of lemon. I find myself in Brunswick Road again. The lights are on in Tash's house, the thin, grey curtains pulled across the window. I can see shapes beyond the curtains. I watch for a while with my engine idling. Then a Landrover Discovery looms behind me, headlights on full beam and I drive away.

After a dinner of fish and chips I call Hannah but her phone is turned off. I text her as well and get no reply. I try again in the morning with the same result. I call Jessica and when she answers I ask if I can speak to Hannah.

"She's out. Walking. I'll give her a message."

"Her phone's off. Is everything okay?"

"She's having a social media break, I think. Something like that."

"She didn't say anything to me."

"Okay."

"Not that … look, I just wondered when she'll be home, that's all."

"We're having dinner together. So about six, I'd say."

"Cheers. Say hi. From me."

"I will."

"How's Jake?"

"Jake's fine."

"Jessica, are you okay?"

"Of course. You woke me, that's all. Still a bit dopey."

"Nothing new there then."

"Ha ha."

We say our goodbyes and ring off.

I'm asleep in front of Sunday Grandstand when Tash knocks at the door. She stands with her hands on her hips, glaring. "Remember me?"

"Hannah's out," I say. "Come in for a minute."

"I don't give a fuck where Hannah is." Her mouth is a thin line. I see the taxi at the curb behind her, engine running. The window is wound down and the driver is watching and listening, unabashed. "You were going to tell her, Nick. I've been waiting. I've called you over and over."

"I'm sorry." I gaze past her shoulder, past the taxi and the houses opposite. The day is impassive, neutral, unconcerned. I try to work out what I feel but I can't.

She looks at me. Her eyes are wide open. Her expression changes and she starts to say something then shakes her head. She touches her mouth. "There's a bit of you missing, I think. It's a big bit, right out of the middle. It's not even your fault. Not really. I hate you, though, Nick. At this moment, I really fucking hate you."

"I know." I look at her too-big sweater and her soft mouth. Her vulnerability hammers at me. I think of her in bed; her eagerness and the taste of her skin. "I know."

"You really don't. You don't have a clue. I was going to make a scene if Hannah was here. I'm glad she's not. You're not worth it. I feel sorry for her." Her hands are held in tight fists by her side and she rocks towards me as she speaks.

"I don't know what I'm doing, Tash. Or who I am. I don't know anything. It's not an excuse. I'm lost."

"You want my pity now?"

"No. I don't want anything. From you. From anyone."

She looks into my face for a long moment. "I'm going back to my folks. Perhaps I'll appreciate them now. Perhaps I won't. Did I ever tell you where they live?" I shake my head. "Good and I've changed my number." She tries to say something else, but can't. She runs to the taxi and slams the door behind her.

"Did you enjoy that?" I say to the driver. He raises a meaty forearm and gives me a mild and disarmingly charming smile. He drives to the end of the road and turns around. I stand on the doorstep as the taxi drives past me, but I don't really see anything at all.

Hannah is home a little before seven. She's tired and we don't speak much. We are still out of synch. There are things I should ask but I can't be bothered. I'm glad when she goes to bed.

Chapter 9

I was in my early twenties when they met. Hannah didn't register at first. She was just one of a stream of girlfriends that Patrick had from his early teens onward. They were mostly young, mostly pretty and shy and none of them lasted for long.

"Good riddance," he'd say with a shrug. "Plenty more where she came from." And he was right, apparently. I didn't get to know any of them. It didn't seem worth it.

But Hannah was, as it turned out, different. My earliest memory of her is brief and banal. She was waiting in the living room of my parent's house as Patrick changed upstairs. I fetched my jacket from the back of a chair. She stood in the middle of the room. When I entered she must have thought I was Patrick because her face became animated and then she realised her mistake and grinned shyly and said, "Hi."

I nodded and said something about being in a hurry and that was that. I remember that her hair was dark and looked freshly cut and that her lipstick was bright red. She wore a pale cardigan. I thought she was less pretty than Patrick's usual dates.

And I *was* in a hurry. I had a date of my own. She was called Kim and she was my first proper girlfriend. She had pale skin and layered, auburn hair and deep green eyes that I lost myself in. I remember that evening her parents were away and I thought I might be able to spend the night with her. I was wrong, as it turned out, and she broke my heart casually, indifferently, six months later.

Patrick passed me as I approached the front door. He wore a leather jacket and too much after shave. He winked. "Tonights the night, is it, little brother?"

I wondered how he knew. I nodded towards the living room. "You're keeping the lady waiting," I said.

Chapter 10

Christmas Day is mild and windy with a hint of rain. Hannah and I sleep in, exchange gifts in bed, kiss hesitantly and briefly. We speak little during the morning. In the past month we've both retreated into our work. This came as a pleasant surprise to Dan. I worked whole weekends to help him keep on top of things and Hannah hadn't complained at all. She's been absorbed by school trips, endless marking, meeting upon meeting. It seems to suit us both not to spend too much time together. Now we have a holiday we can't avoid and neither of us is entirely sure what to say or do.

It's raining when we park in Dereham Road. My mother watches from the door as we scuttle towards the house. She kisses Hannah's cheek. Hannah doesn't flinch, which I consider mildly heroic. We exchange presents and "Happy Christmas's". My mother is trying hard to keep smiling. Her voice is light, if wavering, yards away from the waspish, accusatory monotone she usually favours. Hannah is grinning and nodding and laughing shrilly. I barely recognise her. I don't know what to do so I try to absorb the unreality of it all; the air of barely restrained hysteria.

I look at the miniature Christmas tree in the living room; the ribbons of tinsel hanging from the ceiling and walls; the dining room table, covered with a deep red cloth, laid with mum's best cutlery and china; the

Christmas crackers and party hats. It doesn't belong in this house. You might as well put a party frock on a corpse.

I consider running; peeling away from the pair of lunatics in their new dresses and their perfume and just running and running.

I realise that Hannah is saying something, jolting me from my reverie. "What?"

"I said, something smells nice."

"All the trimmings," my mother says.

"Great," I say.

"I mean, it's not easy, on a pension."

"Sausage and mash would've been fine."

"Nick," Hannah says.

"What?"

"It's alright, dear," my mother says. "He likes his little jokes, does Nicholas. As I'm sure you know. My advice? Never have children. Have I told you about the time …"

Her voice drifts off as she guides Hannah into the kitchen. I wait a couple of minutes before following them. It's almost dark outside and the dining room curtains are drawn. Two standard lamps in opposite corners supply the light but they aren't enough and the room seems to consist more of shadow than of anything else.

In the kitchen my mother pours us mercifully small glasses of sweet sherry and tells us that dinner will be about twenty minutes. She checks the oven, chats whilst she makes gravy. Actually chats. She asks Hannah about her parents and about Jessica and sounds as though she gives a shit.

Shortly she shoos us into the dining room. Hannah and I sit opposite each other. "She's making an effort," Hannah says. "You could at least do the same."

"Believe me, I am."

A minute later my mother bursts through the dining room door carrying a huge serving plate crammed with a roast turkey and a miscellany of vegetables. It actually smells pretty good.

"Dinner is served," she says, planting it on the table between us. It's probably as close as she will ever get to a flourish.

I stand as I carve and they both watch me. I try to imagine my father at this same table, doing the same thing. I can't. My mother holds her plate out to me. She looks younger, I think, in her new dress and with some make up on for once. Her expression is rapt. She catches my glance and something sly slides across her face.

"What?" I say.

"Nothing." The slyness has gone but, the smile that is left is thin and meaningless.

I feel giddy suddenly, as though everything is tilting. "What?" I say again. Hannah's eyes narrow. I put the carving knife on the table. I hear the front door open. "Shit," I say.

"Sorry I'm late, mum," Patrick says as he shoves the dining room door open. He has a present in one hand, his coat over an arm. Then he sees Hannah and he stops dead.

Mum sits with her arms folded, her mouth a thin line.

Hannah stands. "You're a bitch," she says quietly. Then, "I'm leaving. Nick?"

"Not yet."

She hesitates. "Okay. Call me when you're ready. I'll pick you up."

"Thanks. I'm sorry, Hannah."

She doesn't look at me. She brushes past Patrick with her head down.

"I had no idea," he says. "Honestly."

"Satisfied," I say.

"I mean it," Patrick says. "I didn't know."

"I wasn't speaking to you." I look at our mother. "Was it worth it? All the trouble you went to?"

She starts loading her plate with turkey and roast potatoes and mashed swede. "Shame to waste it." I snatch the plate from her and throw it onto the floor. "You'll clear that up before you go," she says.

Patrick hasn't moved. I ask him how he'd got here.

"She got me a taxi. I'm sorry."

"It's not your fault," I say.

"I just wanted the family together for one last Christmas before I die," my mother says. "Is that so much to ask?"

I keep my eyes on Patrick. He looks pale and old and lost. No matter what he's done in the past I don't want to hurt him any further. "Yes. It is. You know it is. You know very well how Hannah feels. And why."

She radiates contempt. "In my day you stood by your husband. No matter what."

Patrick speaks quietly. "The way you did with dad."

"What?" I say.

"Nothing," Patrick says.

My mother's face goes momentarily blank then her expression sharpens again and she points at me. "I nearly died for you. Giving birth. Nearly bled to death."

"Not this again," I say. The familiar litany, repeated mantra-like since I'd been old enough to understand it.

"So ungrateful," she says, gathering herself, picking at the turkey carcass.

"But it's not actually true, is it?" We both look at Patrick. "Dad told me. Both our births were dead simple. Like shelling peas, the midwife said."

"That's rubbish." But her voice wavers.

"Why didn't you mention this before?" I say to Patrick.

He opens his mouth, then closes it again.

A little later I stand in the back garden. Patrick joins me. The rain has stopped but the cloud is low and sulphurous and the air is warmer than it should be. The garden is short and featureless, half grass, half paving stones.

"What did you get her?"

"What?"

"Mum. For Christmas."

"Oh. A jumper. The witch."

"What's she doing?"

"Washing up. She's whistling to herself." He wears his battered leather jacket over a thick navy sweater.

"I won't be back, you know. Ever."

"So you say."

"I mean it."

He's quiet for a moment. "Maybe. You *have* changed."

"Thank Christ for that."

After a small silence he says, "Did you see Hannah's face when she walked past me? The hatred on it?"

"She didn't even look at you."

"I saw it though."

"It wasn't for you. Not this time."

"Still ..."

"I think you've got to let that go, Patrick."

"Yeah. Easily said. She hates me though, doesn't she?" I don't look at him, don't speak. "But you don't?"

"Don't what?"

"Hate me."

"No." He nods. I pull a creased cheque from the wallet in my back pocket and hand it to him. "Christmas present. I didn't expect to be giving this to you today, but still."

He reads the amount. "I thought you were broke?"

"I am. Had a bit of a sort out, though."

"Are you gambling again?"

I half-laugh. "No."

"I don't know when I'll be able to pay you back."

"It doesn't matter."

"Thanks. And … I'm sorry."

"I know."

"Not just today …"

"I know," I say again.

We leave our mother in the kitchen. She's drinking sherry and listening to the radio. The house stinks of the food she's cooked. It seems to be spoiling already. Her cheeks are red, her eyes clear and defiant and she says nothing at all as we slam the front door behind us and set off in search of a pub that is still open.

Patrick stands at the bar of the *Earl of Leicester* as I take a call from Hannah. "Do you want picking up yet?" she asks.

"No. I'll walk."

"Is Patrick still with you?"

"Yes."

"I see. How's he getting home?"

"I haven't thought that far ahead yet."

"I'll go to Jessica's for tonight. Patrick can stay at ours, but I want him gone in the morning."

"Okay."

"You were right about today."

"A stopped clock and all that."

Her voice changes. "You sound ... what's wrong, Nick?"

"How long have you got?"

"What?"

"Nothing. We've got to talk tomorrow, Hannah."

A pause, then, "I know."

I break the connection as Patrick slams a pint in front of me. "Trouble in paradise?" he says. His smile freezes as he sees the expression on my face. "Sorry. Cheap shot."

I thank him for the beer. The bar is emptying out, leaving a hard core of florid-faced, middle-aged men and us. Patrick asks if I'm hungry. Neither of us has eaten since breakfast. "I suppose I should be," I say. "But I'm not."

It turns out Patrick isn't either, but he feels we should have something, what with the drinking and everything, so he buys us a packet of crisps each. He picks at his for a moment then pushes the bag aside.

"I can't believe she did that," he says.

"You can't believe it? Really? I knew she was up to something. I tried to warn ..."

"Perhaps she's lonely."

"Lonely?"

"She hasn't got many friends ..."

"She hasn't got *any* friends, Patrick. It's what comes of being a borderline fucking sociopath."

"She's still our mother."

"Jesus."

"Look ... she's had a hard life ..."

"Has she? How would I know? How would *you* know, come to that? International woman of fucking mystery that she is. Mind you, you've got twelve years on me. Perhaps you do know. Maybe you've got the whole family tree mapped out, you just never bothered to tell me."

"It's not like that. You know it isn't."

"I don't *know* anything. That's the point."

"You're whining again. I thought you'd changed."

"Fuck me." I drain my pint in two swallows and order another.

"Did you ever think I may be protecting you, Nick? Did that never occur to you?"

"No. Frankly. You bullied me, Pat. You were bigger and stronger and you bullied me like you bullied everyone."

"You made it too easy."

"Bullshit."

"I resented you, it's true. I never wanted a little brother. Who does?"

"I think I worked that out a long time ago."

We sit and drink in silence for a while as the closeness that we'd stumbled upon at our mother's house unravels. When our glasses are empty I say, "You can stay at ours tonight. Hannah's at Jessica's."

"Mum paid for a taxi both ways. Thanks, though."

As he stands I say, "What about Dad?"

"What about him?"

"You had ten years with him."

"I know. I can count." He shrugs his jacket on.

"What did I have?" I know I'm whining again and I see the irritation on his face. "Nothing. Not even a photo. I mean, I've tried the internet, but I don't even know his real name."

"I wouldn't bother, Nick."

"Just tell me. Give me something."

"There's not much to know."

"That's it? Five words?"

"I was only ten. I don't remember much." He

makes his way to the door. "They were good match, though. Mum and Dad. I can tell you that." I follow him as he makes his way onto the street. "Happy Christmas," he says without looking back. I watch him as he walks away from me.

Chapter 11

A fortnight after Kim dumped me I was in my bedroom, listening to Elliot Smith, drenched with self-pity and trying desperately not to dwell on Kim and her bottomless eyes.

Patrick burst in without knocking. This wasn't unusual. "Double date. That's what you need."

"What?"

"Double date? I take it you're familiar with the concept? Two couples …"

"Yeah, yeah. Get to the point, Patrick. I'm not in the mood."

"Hannah has a sister," Patrick said.

"Hannah and her Sisters," I said. Patrick looked blank. "It's a film. Woody Allen. Years old now."

"Whatever. Anyway, her sister's called Jessica. Hannah wants us to go out. As a four."

"Why?"

"Jessica's a bit low. Hannah seems to think that you're … nice."

"We've barely spoken."

"Probably why she likes you. Thing is, Jessica's hot. Not that you heard that from me. Obviously."

"Obviously."

"So, are you in?"

"I dunno."

"Come on. Do you good. Stop you moping around."

"Hannah keen, is she?"

"Seems to be."

"And what Hannah wants, Hannah gets, right?"

"It's not like that. I'm not under the thumb."

"Pretty serious, though. It's been what, six months? Close to a personal best."

"There is something about her." He was briefly quiet. "I'm going to ask her to marry me."

"What the fuck?" For a moment the customary cockiness fled from my brother's expression and body language and he seemed younger somehow, almost vulnerable. "Does Mum know?"

His face hardened again. "No. And not a word, little brother. To anyone."

"Scout's honour."

"She doesn't like Hannah."

"I'd noticed. To be fair, she doesn't like anyone."

He grunted. "True enough. I'll be out of here soon, though. Thank God. No offence."

"None taken."

"You could get out too. Nothing stopping you. You could get a place with Richard or something."

"Maybe."

He waited for me to continue but I didn't. The crescendo of Elliott Smith's *Bled White* filled the silence. "Anyway, Saturday, yeah? Pictures, pub, club."

"No clubs. I don't do clubs."

He laughed and looked me up and down. "And try and make yourself presentable. It's a big ask, I know, but …"

"Whatever," I said.

Chapter 12

Hannah is home by mid-morning on Boxing Day. She slings her overnight bag on the kitchen table, piles her coat and scarf on top of it. "Jessica sends her love."

"That's nice. How's Jake?"

"I think you were right about Jake."

"Is Jessica still besotted?"

"No. Not that she'll admit it."

"Your sister? Stubborn? Who'd have believed it?"

She looks at me for the first time since she walked in. "We've got to talk, you said. Are we talking yet?"

"No. Not really."

"I'm tired."

"Me too."

"I didn't sleep well last night."

"Same."

Her hair is held in place by a crimson scrunchie. She releases it, tosses it on top of her coat and scarf. She pulls at her hair absently then lets it drop to her shoulders. I remember the times I'd watched her, waiting for her expression to change. Now there is no expression at all. This is how things end, I think.

She catches me staring at her. Her smile is a reflex, gone almost before I've registered it. "Some Christmas, huh?"

"I'm sorry about yesterday. About Patrick."

"Not your fault. You mum did quite a number on me."

"She almost had me fooled."

"Almost. The hatred in that woman. It takes my breath away."

"Yeah, it's pretty solid, isn't it? Not much room for anything else, I think."

"There must have been once? Presumably?"

"One would hope."

"You don't care?"

"No, Hannah," I say. "I don't."

"Fine," she says, letting out a long breath. We both look at the kettle, but we stay where we are, at either end of the kitchen table, both wary, tensed, waiting for the other to say something that matters.

"Patrick didn't stay here last night, did he? I think I'd have known if he had. I'd have smelt him, sensed him."

"No, he didn't stay. He's changed, I think. Or he's trying to, at least."

"It's my turn not to care."

"He's sorry."

"He told you that?"

"Yes."

"You think maybe he should be apologising to me?"

"Would you listen?"

"No." A beat, then, "I brushed past him yesterday and it made my skin crawl. When I got back here I had to take a shower."

"I'm sorry. He can't change that now. But I think he would if he could."

"Well, bully for him." She pulls a chair free from under the table. Its feet shriek on the tiled floor. She sits on it, props her elbows on the table, looks at me. "So, Nick? Are we talking yet?"

"No. This is small talk. You know it is."

She nods once. "I can't do it here, though. Do you know what I mean?"

"Yes."

"Well, the sales are on."

"Sales?"

"You know. Shopping. A girl's best friend."

"You want to go shopping?"

"Have you got a better idea?"

I admit that I haven't.

Hannah buys a blouse and a pair of shoes. We're in John Lewis when she chooses the blouse and she holds it up against her chest and asks for my opinion. I say it looks good, it suits her. She smiles and goes to pay for it. I want to scream. I buy a shirt from Slater's that I neither want nor need and then we make our way to *Café Nero*, pick up a couple of lattes and sit on the high chairs by the window opposite Lloyd's bank.

"I prefer *Starbucks*," Hannah says. She looks awkward, perched on the chair, knees pointing towards the window. I nearly say, we'll go to *Starbucks* next time, but I stop myself.

"At least you can taste the coffee here," I say. She makes a face. Music, something light and jazzy, plays in the background. No Christmas songs, thankfully. The staff, at the bar to our left, are young and keen and noisy and their laughter and the sounds of the machines they use to make their various coffees and smoothies washes over the music and the soft babble of conversation.

Hannah puts her hands together as though in prayer, then balances her chin on her fingertips. "This is hard," she says.

"Isn't it just." I watch a young couple scuttle for cover from a sudden shower that snaps at the pavement beyond the window.

"I'm seeing someone," Hannah says. "Have been for a while."

"I know."

"Oh."

"I mean, I'd gathered as much. I haven't been stalking you or anything. I don't know who it is, although I'd guess it's a teacher."

"I see."

"Am I right?"

"Actually, he's not a teacher. He's a parent. Of one of the kids in my class."

"A parent? Wow. Anyone I know?"

"No."

"Fair enough." I drink some coffee and wipe foam from my upper lip. I feel Hannah's eyes on me.

"Don't you want to know his name? How long it's been going on?"

"Not particularly."

"Don't you care?"

"It all comes back to caring."

"What?"

"Of course I care. I look at you sometimes and … you're still beautiful, is what I mean. But what does it matter? I mean it hurts like fuck. Does that help? If I sat here crying, if I declared my undying love for you, would that change anything?"

"It might."

"Come on, Hannah. It's hard, facing things. I get that, believe me. I'm great at *not* facing things. Top class. One of the best, really. But sometimes … well … here we are."

"Jesus, Nick." Her eyes are becoming wet. I think that mine are too.

"Things end. We're not special. Not immune."

"Who said anything about endings?"

"Right."

"I said I was seeing someone. Not that I loved him."

"And you love me, do you?"

She hesitates just a fraction. Just enough. "Of course I do."

Outside the rain has stopped. It's getting dark now. "I don't think you do. I don't think you ever did." She starts to speak but I hold up a hand. "And that's fine. Really. I think you needed me for a while. And perhaps I needed you."

"You're speaking in riddles."

"You needed me to get away from Patrick. I understand that. I was a kind of bridge. A bridge from Patrick back to normal people."

"Nick? You're scaring me. It's as though you had this all worked out. Your little speeches." Her voice is rising slightly, her fingers sliding up and down the sides of her white porcelain coffee cup.

I tell her about Tash.

After a while she blinks hard twice. Her smile is a bitter, brittle thing that doesn't last long. "Well, then. We're even, aren't we?"

"So you have slept with him?" She nods slowly and starts to say something but I interrupt her. "Don't tell me his name. I don't want to know his name. Not yet."

"You are a bastard," she says softly.

"You don't know the half of it."

A hardness settles in her eyes. "You'd better tell me, then."

There's no way to sugar-coat it. "I've taken out a second mortgage."

"The house is in both of our names!"

"I know it is."

"How much?" I tell her. "Jesus Christ. And you forged my signature to get it?"

"Yes."

"When?"

"Last week."

She takes a long breath and stares into the depths of her coffee cup. "You're gambling, then?"

"I was. I'm not now."

"Right."

"I don't expect you to believe me."

"Probably just as well."

"I'm not begging for forgiveness. I don't expect any. I'm just telling you what I've done."

"Thanks."

"You'd rather I didn't?"

"I'd rather you hadn't done any of it in the first place. And even if I accept that you're not gambling, which I don't, you admit that you were, whilst promising me the opposite?"

"Yes."

"I can see why you'd think that we were over."

"I'm not making any excuses."

"Big of you."

"I'm sorry about the loan, your signature. It was the only way to keep the business afloat. I'll pay it all back. I promise."

"You promise?"

"Of course, you can take it to a solicitor. Or we can factor it into the separation."

"Factor it in?" Hannah's eyes are wide open. She looks as though I've slapped her. "I don't know what to say to you, Nick. Honestly." Her voice trembles.

"I'm sorry. I really am. I know I seem cold, detached. It's the only way I can get through this. I'll find a flat. It could take a while, though. It's not a great time of year. I hoped I could use the spare room until then."

Hostility flares in her expression then dies quickly. "Of course. Whatever. You've got it all worked out. Will you get a place with her?"

"I told you, that's over."

"You told me? Well, that's all right, then."

"Hannah."

"Sorry. Am I a little sharp? Please excuse me. It's not been the best Christmas ever. Do you know what I mean?"

I close my eyes. When I open them again Hannah is crying. A waitress asks if she can take our cups. Then she sees Hannah's face and apologises and backs away.

"Shall we get back to the car?" I say.

Hannah nods, her face in her hands. I try to take her arm, but she pushes me away as we walk to the door.

The Christmas lights and decorations adorning the market and Jarrold's department store shine brightly in the darkness. We make our way to the car in silence.

Chapter 13

I don't remember what film we saw. I think we ended up in the *Walnut Tree Shades* in the city centre. I know I had by far the best of the deal. Hannah was all right, I thought. Pleasant enough, but quiet, distant almost. Jessica hummed with unfocused energy. She laughed constantly at my jokes and kept touching my shoulder, my arm. The music in the pub was loud and Jessica had to lean close and press her mouth against my ear so that I could hear her. Her breath was warm and made me shiver. I remember the feel of her breast on my arm. I found that I stopped thinking about Kim.

Patrick was quiet too. I caught him looking at me a couple of times during the evening but his expression was unreadable. He drank steadily to no obvious effect. Hannah sipped wine then orange juice. Jessica worked her way through bottled beers, gin and tonics, a handful of lurid cocktails.

Despite my reservations we went onto a nightclub on Prince of Wales Road. Hannah and Patrick hadn't been particularly keen either but Jessica's energy overwhelmed us. The club was hot and packed and tacky. A vast silver glitter ball hung from the ceiling. Of course it did. The dance floor was on three different levels. The music was incomprehensively loud. Jessica insisted that I dance with her. Her cheeks were cherry-red and her eyes shone with an odd light. Eventually the music slowed and something ballady came on. I slumped against her. My legs ached and my shirt felt glued to my back.

"Too much for you?" Jessica said.

"Something like that." My breathing slowed. I held onto her narrow waist. My face was in her hair, which smelled acrid. When my mouth brushed against it I tasted something chemical.

"My boyfriend dumped me last week," Jessica said as she pressed against me.

"You sure he didn't die of exhaustion?"

She pulled away and looked into my face. "You're meant to say, what a fool he must be. Something like that."

"I thought that was obvious."

"Mmm."

Patrick and Hannah sat at a corner table. He was speaking animatedly, his eyes on Hannah. She studied the bottom of her empty glass and nodded occasionally.

I closed my eyes and nuzzled Jessica's neck. It was mostly to get away from the taste and smell of her hair, but she murmured something and squeezed closer against me. The music was sultry and low.

After a while I felt a hand on my shoulder. "We're off," Patrick said. I nodded. His expression was blank. Hannah smiled at me and touched my arm.

After they'd gone Jessica said, "At least you'll stop looking at her now."

"Who?"

"Hannah." There was a break in the music and she eased herself away from me. I was surprised by the sullenness in her voice. "You couldn't keep your eyes off her."

"I don't think so."

She pulled further away from me, then put a hand to her mouth and her expression changed. "I've got to get outside, Nick." Her eyes were wide open. "Now." She turned and tried to run for the door, high heels clip-clopping on the wooden dance floor. A pair of burly doorman parted for us and I saw their irritated amusement as we passed. Then we were outside. It was August and the air was warm and thick. It was past midnight I think and the street was busy. Jessica just about made it around the corner, into an alleyway, before vomiting copiously onto a pile of black plastic rubbish bags. I stood next to her and watched her spasm. She wore a sparkly, purple top that caught the moonlight and multiplied it. I didn't know what to do. She seemed to pause. She was still bent over and her breathing was ragged. I put a hand on her shoulder. "Fuck off," she said weakly. I thought she was going to say something else, but instead she started puking again.

I backed off a little, leant back against the wall, breathed in the velvet, peppery air and waited.

"I'm sorry," she said a few minutes later. She stood by my side. Her face was bone-white, her eyes red-rimmed and damp.

"Are you okay?"

"Do I look it?"

"Do you want an honest answer?"

She laughed. "Not really. Some date, huh?"

"I had a good time."

"I'm not usually like this."

"It's fine. Shall we take a walk? Find ourselves a taxi?"

"But the night is young."

"Not for us it isn't."

She laughed again and took my arm.

*

She'd cleaned herself up a little but I could still smell the puke on her. We walked past a fried chicken place and the colour that had started to grow in her cheeks fled again. "Christ. This is all Gavin's fault."

"The guy who dumped you?"

"It sucks being dumped."

"Sure does."

"I'm sorry … I know … I mean, Hannah said …"

"That's fine. Water under the bridge and all that."

"Well, I think she's silly, whoever she is. For what it's worth."

"Thanks, Jessica. I think Gavin's silly too."

"Aww," she said, her head nudging against my shoulder. "Aren't we just adorable?"

A hen party eddied past, all borderline hysteria and too much flesh. "Speaking of Hannah," I said, "Why did you think I was looking at her?"

"Dunno. Just used to it, I suppose."

"Really?"

"You've already flattered me, Nick, no need to overdo it."

"Seriously. I mean, she's nice and everything, but …" I let the sentence trail away.

"Your brother seems besotted."

"I suppose he does. As far as Patrick is ever besotted with anything."

"I wonder if he's asked her to marry him yet."

"You know about that?"

"Hannah's expecting it. She'll say yes, of course."

"Of course?"

"Mostly because it'll piss our parents off."

"Really?"

"Really. She's not as sweet as she looks. And our folks *are* a pain in the arse."

"Are they so bad?"

She raised a hand and ticked the points off one finger at a time. "They're cold, controlling and petty. And they're rabid Tories, which we're not. Well, I'm not, I'm not sure what Hannah is."

"Fair enough. Families eh?"

"I think Larkin had it right."

"I think he probably did." We walked in a companionable silence for a while. "So, Patrick? Your parents not big fans, then?"

"Hardly. They can't stand him. He's not good enough for their little Princess." She screwed her face up. "No offence."

"Absolutely none taken. To be fair, they're probably right."

She nudged me. "That's not very loyal."

"Loyal? No. Patrick." I let my voice become lilting and high-pitched. "He's my brother and I love him." Jessica stifled a laugh. "Anyway, loyalty? The way you talk about your sister?"

"Hannah," she said, mimicking my silly voice of a moment ago. "She's my sister and I love her."

"Funny thing, love."

"So they tell me."

"Families," I said again. "If you're really lucky I'll tell you about my mum some time."

"Promise?"

"Be careful what you wish for."

"It'd mean we'd see each other again."

"There's that," I said, sliding an arm around her waist.

Chapter 14

It takes until the first week in February to find myself a flat. The preceding month has been a chilly hinterland; Hannah and I avoid each other as much as possible and what meetings we have are wreathed with an excruciating, icy formality. We decide to try and manage without solicitors, for as long as possible, at least. This is against the advice of Hannah's parents. The disentanglement of our lives begins with brief, bleak discussions. We agree on tiny, bland things, edging away from each other with baby steps. The day that I move out Hannah gets up very early and leaves for work without saying goodbye.

Dan helps me move. I'm using the money I've borrowed against our house to set myself up in my own place and to stabilise the business. I show Dan the books, tell him I'm willing to continue to help with any paperwork, but the business is his now and his alone. He is wary, understandably so, but not unhappy.

There isn't much to move, it only takes a couple of trips in his transit. Without work to bitch and snipe about we don't have much in common so the conversation is limited. It's early evening when we finish and what light is left is whisky-coloured and fading. He shakes my hand and wishes me luck. We should have a drink sometime, he says, but his eyes slide away from mine as he speaks. I tell him that I'm sure that we will and then he leaves and I'm alone in my new home.

It's a one bedroom flat, ground floor, purpose built, in a cul-de-sac off Christchurch Road. The front door leads out from the living room onto a tiny garden and then the street. The walls need a fresh coat of paint and the central heating is noisy and unreliable. I think of Patrick's place near King's Lynn; at least mine *has* central heating. It's cosy enough. It'll do.

I've paid the rent for six months and I've got about that long before my money runs out, even allowing for whatever Dan pays me for doing his paperwork. I need to find a job. I've promised Hannah that I'll pay her back the money I've borrowed. As I sit on a packing box and watch the darkness fall through a curtainless window, neither of these occurrences seem especially likely.

Only Hannah and Dan know where I live. I haven't seen or spoken to Patrick or my mother since Christmas. I have no idea where Tash is and even less idea if I care. It occurs to me that I have nobody left to hurt. I feel deeply lonely. A wave of exquisite self-pity courses through me.

For the next fortnight time passes as though weighted with lead. It snows solidly for three days and for a further week the temperature barely crawls above freezing. There's no horse racing in the UK for a number of days and it's probably just as well. The need to gamble has become a crawling, visceral thing. I feel it in my gut, twisting and roiling, rending me fevered and limp. A fantasy forms; I have enough cash for six months, so if I stick it all on an even money shot and it wins then I can manage for a year. And if it loses? Well, there are high buildings and railway tracks and many other ways to seek oblivion should it come to that. There is nobody left to hurt, after all.

I eat little. I drink only water. I leave the heating off for as long as possible for no obvious reason. If I possessed a hair shirt I would undoubtedly wear it. I think of Hannah often, Jessica sometimes, Tash occasionally. I listen to Jeff Buckley and Elliott Smith and Aimee Mann. I let Patrick and my mother wallow in my subconscious along with all the other crap. I tell myself every evening, in the tones of the sanctimonious prick that I am, that a day without gambling is a good day. I sleep surprisingly well.

Late one morning in the middle of February Jessica calls. I have my phone turned off most of the time. Whenever I switch it on I groan inwardly at the thought having to negotiate a slew of messages. I never get any, which kind of serves me right, I suppose.

Her call comes as a genuine surprise. I'm halfway through a paperback, one of a multitude that I've picked up from charity shops and flea markets. It is entirely unremarkable and I'll forget the plot as soon as I've read it.

I pick up the phone and stare at it as the call tone plays and Jessica's name displays on the screen. I let it go to voicemail but she doesn't leave a message. If she had then perhaps I'd ignore it but I'm intrigued so I call her back.

"Hey," she says. Her voice sounds shocking and real and I realise that I've barely spoken to anyone for a fortnight. After a moment she says, "You there?"

"Yes," I say. "Sorry, you woke me up."

"Look, I hear you've got your own place. You didn't even tell me. That fucking hurts, I've got to tell you."

I think she's probably joking but I'm not really sure. "I'm sorry, I …"

Her laugh is a crackly bark though the phone's speaker. "I'm kidding."

"Of course."

"But I am in the neighbourhood. You fancy some lunch?"

"I don't know, Jessica, I haven't really …"

"Hey, I've got sandwiches, too much for one. I'll be there in ten."

She hangs up and I look stupidly at the phone for several moments.

"You look like shit," she says, when I open the door.

"I suppose Hannah gave you my address."

"Of course. Was it meant it to be a secret?"

"No, but …"

"Let me in, why don't you? It's freezing out here."

She's carrying a *Pret a Manger* paper bag and she takes it through to the kitchen.

"I'd give you the tour," I say, from the living room, "but you've pretty much just had it."

"Cosy," she says. I hear her rattling around in a cupboard, finding some plates.

"Make yourself at home, why don't you?"

"Cheers." I hear a drawer open then close again.

She brings the food through; a variety of sandwiches cut into tiny triangles, some posh-looking crisps decanted into a bowl. Then she passes me a small plate and napkin and a bottle of fruit juice. She shrugs off her coat and gloves and scarf and lays them on the sofa, then, with a sigh, plants herself in the elderly, but comfortable, armchair that I usually favour.

"Thanks," I say.

"You're welcome." She reaches for a sandwich, then pauses and points at my face. "What's that?"

I run my fingers instinctively through the stubble on my chin. "It's a beard."

"No, it isn't. Whatever it is, it's got to go."

"I think it's rugged."

"It isn't rugged. You look like a twat. Shave it off, please."

"It's so good to see you, Jessica."

Actually it is. Her proximity is almost overwhelming compared to the wintry, monochrome world to which I've consigned myself. She seems vivid and hyper real in a bright pink sweater and neat blue jeans. She smells wonderful too. I try to recall the last time I've showered or used deodorant. Three days? Four? Something like that. I feel self-conscious and struggle to hide it.

We eat and it's good. I'm hungrier than I realised and I finish eating long before Jessica.

"I think you needed that."

"I think I did."

She wipes her fingers on a paper napkin and drains her juice. "Good Christmas?"

That makes me laugh. "Awesome. Yours?"

"Better than yours, I reckon."

"That's a pretty low bar. Look, I'm sorry about Christmas, not getting together, Hannah wanted to, but ..."

"It's okay. You had a lot going on," she says mildly. "The last time we met was that Thai meal? Do you remember?"

"Seems like a lifetime ago."

"A lot of water under a lot of bridges since then."

"How *is* Jake?"

"Jake's history." She gathers the plates together, her eyes averted.

"I'm sorry."

"No, you're not."

"No. I'm not. You're too good for him."

She stands and I follow her into the kitchen. "This sink could do with a scrub," she says as she plants the plates on the draining board. "And the floor."

"I'll get someone in. Give the place a once over."

"You lazy bastard. You could actually do it yourself, you know."

"It's a thought," I say. "I'm not sure it'll catch on."

She leans back against the sink. She wears a simple silver chain around her throat and she plays with it briefly then folds her arms in front of her chest. "I'm living with Hannah."

"How the hell did that happen?"

"Jake left, my lease expired, I quit my job. Things got … chaotic."

"Perhaps on reflection your Christmas wasn't that much better than mine."

"It's a close run thing."

"We're in the same boat then, pretty much."

"I'd say you're ahead on points." She spreads her arms wide. "You have this palace, after all."

"But you still have your car."

"What happened to yours?"

"Sold it. Needed the funds. Call it a draw?" I vaguely remember saying something similar to her once before, in a different time, a different context.

"Neck and neck in the misery stakes. How wonderful."

"You don't seem miserable."

She pushes herself away from the sink and faces me. "I'm not. I'm fine. It was never going to work with Jake, not really and I can put up with Hannah for a bit. And work …" She scrunches up her face. "How many jobs have I been through since uni?" I start to say something but she holds up a hand. "It's a rhetorical question. I hated working in Diss. I'll find something in Norwich. Not a problem. I interview well."

"Must be your natural charm."

"That must be it. And you?"

"Me, what?"

"What are your plans? Are you being a good boy?"

"I'm not gambling, if that's what you mean." She raises her eyebrows a fraction. "I'm really not. It's been months now."

"That's good. Well done."

"That sounded really patronising, Jessica."

"It wasn't meant to."

"Okay. My plan ... get through the winter, find a job, don't gamble."

"Simple."

"A simple plan for a simple man."

I wait for her to contradict me but she doesn't.

I'm sad when she leaves, but I try to hide it. "Thanks for the food," I say at the door.

"No problem."

"My treat next time." She smiles and starts to head for her Nissan Micra. "I suppose you knew?" I say.

She pauses. "About what?"

"Hannah's ... friend."

"Steve?"

"I didn't really want to know his name."

"Of course I knew."

"Of course."

"I couldn't ... she's still my sister, Nick."

"I know ... I'm not ... I just wondered, that's all."

She doesn't say anything for a moment. She's wrapped up tight against the cold and her breath plumes around her face. "I've really got to go. Get inside, for goodness sake. You'll freeze your bits off out here."

"Yes, boss." I watch her back as she leaves, then go inside. The flat seems drab and empty without her.

Chapter 15

A week after our first date we went to a gig at the Waterfront. Some local band I barely remember. Jessica was calmer, a little more muted. She drank less. She said later that she was trying to impress me, which I found oddly touching.

In those days there was a wine bar around the corner from the Waterfront. It was nice enough, but it was always quiet and it didn't last long. It was ideal for us on that particular evening; we sat in a corner, in candlelight, nursing a bottle of Pinot Grigio, heads tilted towards each other. It sounds romantic, but it wasn't. It was intimate, though; perhaps too intimate and maybe we shared too much too soon and that was why we didn't last long. It felt adult and exhilarating at the time. For my part, I suppose, that was because for once I was being honest. Mostly. Even in my early twenties I was an inveterate liar. Even before I was an addict. In our household, the way we were brought up, truth was currency and I learned to hoard it, to keep it to myself. I didn't lie to deceive, particularly. I just felt that the truth was no one else's business.

Jessica disarmed me, two sips in. "We're damaged, Hannah and I."

I took a mouthful of wine myself, playing for time. "So much for small talk."

"Do you want small talk?"

I think that I probably did, but what could I say? "Of course not."

"Most people do. I think Gavin did."

"I'm not Gavin. Why are you damaged?"

"I don't know. That's the thing, isn't it? When you grow up, when you meet people, you realise that this little world you've been cocooned in, it isn't ..."

"What?"

"I was going to say normal. But what's normal?"

"Good question. We're talking parents, I take it?"

"Back to Larkin. But, yeah. Basically." She must have seen something in my face because she put a hand up suddenly and said, "God no. Not *that*. Just to make it clear, I mean Mum and Dad are *fucking* mental, but they never ... he never ..."

"I didn't say anything, Jessica."

"I know, but it's the obvious ..."

"I wasn't thinking that. Honestly," I lied.

"Okay." She gave a brittle giggle. "I kind of asked for it, though." She reached a hand out absently and laid it over mine. "It's so hard with this stuff; finding a way in."

"Just say it."

"Just say it." Her fingertips were cool against my skin. "Okay."

Turns out her Dad had a breakdown and her Mum was a drunk. Not so unusual, not really, not in the scheme of things, and I suppose I felt a small sense of anti-climax after the big build-up. I hid it, though; at least I thought I did.

"I know, right? Big deal. People have breakdowns, people drink too much."

"I don't think ..."

"It's okay, Nick. I get it. It's not even that. Families cope with stuff like that, pull together. They do on TV, at least." She took a tiny sip of wine and coiled her fingers against the stem of the glass. "It's the denial." Her eyes closed very slowly, as though they were too heavy for her. When she opened them again they were suddenly too wide and she looked ever so slightly deranged. "When he was first sick – I was about twelve, I think – he was off work for six months. For most of it he was catatonic, a zombie."

"I'm sorry."

"Hey, it happens. Depression. We saw the prescriptions, heard Mum and the GP whispering in the kitchen. I didn't really understand, not at twelve, but Hannah explained. She was nice, then. Kind. She held my hand."

"It must have been hard."

"The thing is, Nick, they told everyone he had cancer."

"Cancer?"

"To Mum and Dad, depression equals weakness and you can't have that."

"Christ."

"It's what they told us as well. I mean, we *knew* it wasn't. We could *see* it wasn't. But ..." She searched for the words. "They sat us down and lied to our faces. The treatment would take a while, they said, but the prognosis was good. It was family business and the matter was closed. I could see Hannah building up to a question but Mum stopped her with a look. It was all acid. It cut Hannah dead. So she shut down. Swallowed the lie. She hasn't questioned it since."

"Seriously?"

"Sometimes I feel like I'm going mad. They've created this whole alternate truth, the three of them. Dad's relapsed a couple of times over the years. I mean it happens, right, with mental health? So out comes the story; the cancer's back. He'll be fine though. A bit more treatment and he'll be fine. And now there are three of them saying it; to work, to friends, to *me*. I *know* they're lying. They *know* I know they're lying."

"Jessica," I said, holding her hand.

"It's okay. And then there's Mum."

"The drinking?"

"Well … the migraines."

"Migraines?" It seemed my main task was to stupidly repeat whatever Jessica said. Which was fine. I could do that.

"To Mum and Dad, addiction equals weakness. And you can't have that." She shot me a grim smile and squeezed my hand. "It isn't every week, but it is every month. I've seen her at three in the afternoon absolutely fucking wasted and then Dad will say to me later, "Best give your mum a little space for a while, she's having one of her migraines"."

"Has Hannah swallowed that as well?"

"Hook, line and sinker. I mean, she knows, but …" She gave a long, helpless shrug. "It's all about appearance. For the three of them. And money and status. It's like they've constructed this massive, brittle, shitty shell …"

"Nice image."

She laughed. "And me with an English degree. Still, cracks are showing. In their shell."

"Patrick?"

"Yeah. I mean, Hannah has played their game but she still fucking hates them. Very pass agg, though, that's Hannah. And Patrick … well, he's tall enough and pretty good looking and he earns decent money, but …"

"Ex-council house, mother's an immigrant. Not good stock."

"Exactly. I'm sorry, I know how that sounds …"

"It's okay. It's not you saying it. Not really."

"I suppose not." She topped up our glasses. Something by Portishead played in the background. *Sour Times*, I think it was. "You know, I didn't really mean to say any of that?"

"Are you glad you did?"

"I think so. It feels like I just took a massive shit."

"That imagery again."

"What can I say, I'm a poet. Anyway, your turn."

I kept it brief. Mum's family came to England after the war, from Poland, via various Eastern and then Western European countries. "We had money, we were fine," she snapped once, when Patrick asked her about it. "We weren't Jews, though," she added, as though that mattered. Apparently it did to her because despite her background she was unapologetically anti-Semitic, anti-immigrant, anti-anything that wasn't white, Anglo-Saxon, narrow-minded and hateful. No matter how I framed it, I could not avoid the conclusion that she was simply a bitter old racist.

The family settled in the Midlands – I don't know where exactly as she never told us, just as she never shared her original family name or the fate of her mother and father and younger brother – where she met our father and it wasn't until three years before my birth that they moved to Norwich.

I have few memories of my Dad and what I do have are misty and unreliable. He died when I was two. A car crash, I was told. Patrick said that Mum hinted that Dad had a mistress and that he was on his way to see her when he died. It was justice, she said. It was all he deserved. And the matter was closed.

"Jesus," Jessica said eventually.

"So what do you reckon?" I said. "Call it a draw?"

*

We lasted three months. When we finished it was a mutual thing. Genuinely mutual. We were sitting in the *Mitre* on Earlham Road, nursing our drinks, not saying much, when we looked at each other and smiled and both knew it was over. No bitterness, no blame. Just a sense of quiet relief on my part. I'm not sure what Jessica felt. For all her apparent transparency she's a difficult person to read. We remained friends, on and off. Perhaps we wouldn't have if it hadn't been for Patrick and Hannah.

They finally married in the spring, a couple of years later. Jessica was a bridesmaid. She wore a long peach dress and had her hair up and her skin seemed to glow as though lit from within. I fancied her like mad that day. We danced together at the reception and kissed briefly, but she pulled away from me and ended the evening with a guy called Rob, one of Patrick's friends. I was surprised how much that hurt.

I danced with Hannah as well. We weren't quite friends at this point, but we'd become more familiar and much more comfortable in each other's company during her and Patrick's long, awkward engagement. I think that day, the evening of her wedding, was the first time I found her attractive. She wore a dress similar to Jessica's only it was bigger, fluffier, frillier. It should have looked absurd, but on Hannah it didn't. At the reception she wore a simple grey trouser suit with a white blouse. She had her hair scraped back and tied in a ponytail. I couldn't take my eyes off her. Patrick saw me looking and smiled.

Our mother wasn't there; she claimed to have had an asthma attack the previous night. Hannah and Jessica's parents *were* there, unfortunately. They were a grey, acerbic presence, brooding at the edges of the day and part of the evening. They didn't bother to hide their contempt for Patrick or me. They simpered over Hannah when she gave them the chance. Jessica they mostly ignored. When they left the reception early few noticed and nobody mourned.

Patrick and Hannah flew to Paris for their honeymoon. Patrick told me he intended to visit some First World War battlefields while he was in France. Poor Hannah, I thought. I felt a pang as they drove off. They had a new house to come back to and it would just be me and mum at Dereham Road. I suppose I could have moved out years ago. I don't know why I didn't. Too much effort, maybe.

The reception was held at a hotel on the Newmarket Road. I remember standing outside the entrance watching the taillights of Patrick and Hannah's car disappear. The day had been warm but it was chillier then with the sun gone. I stood and shivered and stuffed my hands deep into my pockets. A few yards away Jessica and Rob giggled and kissed. I was about as lonely as I had ever been. Which was saying something.

Chapter 16

A couple of days after my visit from Jessica I get a text from her sister. Ten words:

When are you going to start paying back my money?

I'm working on it, I reply. I'd done a cursory sweep of the local jobs online earlier that morning so it wasn't completely untrue.

When my phone rings a few minutes later I think it must be Hannah. I brace myself for a bollocking or threats of legal action, but when I pick up the phone it isn't her at all. I don't recognise the number so I let it go to voicemail. I activate the message and listen.

"Hey, it's Richard." After an awkward moment he adds, unnecessarily, even after all these years, "Butler. Do you want to give me a ring back? It's about your brother."

I delete the message. I throw the phone onto the sofa and stare at it. Then I pick it up again and return Richard's call.

"That was quick."

"How's it going?"

"Fantastic. You?"

"You mentioned Patrick?"

"Yeah, look, can we meet up?"

I hesitate. "I suppose. You could come here."

"Where's here?"

I tell him. He says he's free this evening and I tell him that's fine.

*

He's a little early, as it turns out, but it isn't as though I'm doing anything else. I usher him in and we look at each other. We don't shake hands.

"You haven't changed," I say, although he has. His waist is thicker, even allowing for the jumper and the chunky overcoat. His hair, on the other hand, has thinned considerably. He'd had thick, dark waves of it once, but what remains is a soft burr clinging gamely to the top of his scalp.

"Well, that's a lie, but thanks." He removes his coat and hands it to me. "You, on the other hand, look exactly the same."

"Is that a compliment?"

"I honestly don't know. I assume that you're still a cunt?"

I laugh. "I think that would be the majority verdict." I fetch a couple of beers. "I hope that's okay," I say, handing him a Beck's.

"It'll do," he says. "I'm hardly a connoisseur."

We sit, him on the sofa, me in my usual armchair, and make ourselves comfortable.

"I heard your dad sold up," I say.

"A couple of years ago. Got an offer from a chain. He bit their hand off. His heart wasn't in it any more, not since …" His voice falters. He takes a sip of his beer and looks carefully at the label on the bottle.

"Since he found out we were stealing from him?"

"Yeah. That."

"I'm sorry," I say.

"Are you?"

"I think I am, actually."

"I'm not. Silly old sod would never believe we weren't in on it together."

"I suppose from his point of view, that kind of makes sense."

"Perhaps. But he wouldn't listen. He never listens."

"Does it matter, Richard? Together or independently, we *did* steal from him."

"It matters. He wouldn't believe me. I was trying to come clean, but he didn't want to know. Called me a liar. Just as well, for you, I suppose."

"Do you think he'd have had me prosecuted? If he'd known we weren't in it together?"

"Maybe. For a while there I thought he was going to shop us both anyway. Turns out that was a step too far, even for him."

"Did you ever pay him back?"

"No. I assume that you haven't."

"No." There was a point when I had been in a position to, but I'd decided against it. Richard doesn't need to know that. "I still might, one day. But there's a bit of a queue."

There's a small silence. Richard drains his beer so I fetch him another. We settle into some small talk; he's working in a call centre at the Broadland Business Park, he says, and lives nearby, in a rented flat, not dissimilar to mine.

"So, what were you doing in a night club in King's Lynn? Long old taxi drive home."

"It's a gay club," he says.

After a moment I say, "I didn't know."

"That's okay, neither did I, not for the longest time. Or I didn't admit it, at least."

"When did you come out?"

"I haven't. Hence a club in King's Lynn and not one of the nicer one's in Norwich."

"I don't get it."

"It's a small city. Word gets around. And my folks … well, you probably remember."

I don't recall much about them at all, but I see no point in telling him that. "Families," I say, and think of Jessica.

"It would have been … life would be even more difficult if they knew. And I have my inheritance to think of. I think I'm just about forgiven for … what we did. But …" He shudders. "Families indeed."

"Which brings us onto Patrick."

"Patrick."

"On the phone, you said …"

"I know what I said." He places his half-empty bottle on the coffee table and leans forward. "The thing is, Nick, I'm worried about him."

It takes me a moment or two to absorb the fact that someone, other than my mother, has expressed concern for Patrick. "Worried? You hated him, back in the day."

"I didn't hate him. He frightened me. Same as he frightened you."

"He hit you, Richard."

"Just the once. And it was only a slap. I probably deserved it."

"No one deserves it."

"Whatever, man. It was a long time ago. Anyway, he could be nice too. Do you remember?" I remember. A slap one day, an ice cream the next. He'd take me to the pictures sometimes, and the football. "We went to that old American airfield once, didn't we? Where was that?" He frowns, clicking his fingers together.

"Seething."

"Seething, that's it. He loved that place, didn't he? He gave us chapter and verse about the bomber crews, how they weren't much older than we were."

"He likes his military history, does Patrick." I think of his honeymoon and trips to French battlefields.

I'd mentioned it to Hannah once and she'd laughed and changed the subject.

"He wasn't all bad, is all. That's what I'm trying to say."

"I don't suppose anyone is. But he's not your brother, Richard."

"I know, I know. It's just …"

A sudden realisation hits me. "You had a crush on him."

"What? Don't be ridiculous." His face reddens quickly.

"It doesn't matter. It's no big deal."

"Thanks for the permission, Nick. Appreciate it."

The conversation has taken a wrong turn. "I'm sorry," I say. He taps the neck of his beer bottle slowly against his front teeth. His expression has become sullen and he won't look at me. "That was out of order. Look … you came here to tell me something, right?" He nods reluctantly. "Why not tell me, then? I'll keep it zipped. Promise."

After a moment's hesitation, he does.

Richard had a friend who lived in King's Lynn and every six weeks or so he'd visit for the weekend and they'd spend Friday and Saturday evenings at *Hector's House*. It's not the Ritz, he says, not even close, but he can be himself for a while and that means more to him than dirty toilets and sticky floors and watered-down, over-priced drinks.

Patrick was at the bar, drinking a coke when Richard saw him. "I did a double take," he says. "It was such a surprise. And at first I thought he was one of punter's, so …"

"Even more of a surprise."

"Indeed. The first thing he said to me was, *I'm not*

gay, I'm working the door. I'm on a break." Richard chuckles. "Nice to see you too, I said. He smiled at that. He's got a nice smile, your brother."

"Okay."

"A bit later I went outside to see him, to have a chat. My friend was otherwise engaged. He's often otherwise engaged; considerably more often than I am, if I'm honest. Patrick was bored; it was a quiet night and I think he was glad of the distraction. He said he'd never have taken me for a faggot. I didn't take offence."

"It's best not to, with Patrick."

"I was pretty drunk. I went on about you, about what you did. I don't remember exactly …"

"I know. He told me, it's fine."

It just came out, he says. Patrick lapped it up, thought it was hilarious. Richard looks awkward as he speaks, averting his gaze, but I don't care. I do wonder, briefly, if Richard, in his outburst to Patrick, had been honest about his own sticky fingers, but quickly realise that I don't care about that either.

At the end of the evening he thought that was that; a drunken catch up with an old acquaintance, nothing more, nothing less. The next time he visited the club, four weeks later, Patrick wasn't there. He thought no more of it, he says, although I wonder about that.

On New Year's Eve he and his friend pitched up to *Hector's House* a little after eleven. "And there he was, on the door, tall, dark and handsome. He looked like shit though. Years older. I told him so as he checked us in. He asked if I wanted a clip around the ear. So far so hilarious, right?"

"Hilarious."

"He was there when I left, a few hours later. I was on my own again. Are you sensing a trend?" I offer the necessary sympathetic smile. "Thing is, Nick, he hugged me. Hard."

"Patrick?"

"Yeah. I mean … I was shocked, right?" But you liked it, didn't you, I think. It's a mean, dark thought and I cut it off at source. "He said it was good to see me. He wouldn't let go, Nick. He smelled a bit, if I'm honest."

"Was he high?"

"I did wonder. But I don't think so. He felt hot, as though he had a fever. He seemed broken. He started to cry, Nick."

"Fucking hell." I've never known Patrick to cry.

"I asked him if he was okay and he pulled away from me and wiped his face and told me to stop being a cunt."

"And he's back."

"Yeah. And no. I asked if he wanted to go for a coffee and a chat. He said, *I'm not gay* and I said, I think I've gathered that, but if you want a coffee, if you want to talk, that's fine. It's up to you."

"That was nice of you."

"Was it?" He sounds genuinely surprised.

"Yes," I say. "It was."

He shrugs. "Anyway, he took me up on it. Surprise, surprise. A couple of times, actually."

"Where did you go?" I say, for the sake of it, as though it matters.

"Some new place in King's Lynn. It's nice, you'd like it."

Would I? And how would you know, I think. "Are you cold?" I say. He doesn't answer. "I'm cold." I stand and turn the heating up. Outside the wind is gathering, probing at windows and doors.

When I'm settled again, he says, "Does he get gays

and priests mixed up, your brother?" I assume that it's a rhetorical question so I say nothing. "It was like a confession, is all. I mean he asked about me a little, for forms sake, but it was mostly unloading." He shifts in his seat. "That's why I didn't have to ask after you earlier. I'd already heard it all from Patrick."

"His version at least."

"Isn't that all any of us have? Our own version. You have to stack them all up, see where they overlap."

"That's deep, man."

"You're taking the piss and perhaps I deserve it. But …"

"But, what?"

"He didn't spare himself."

"Or me?"

"This isn't about you, Nick," he says gently. "Not everything is."

"Another illusion shattered." I try to keep my voice light, but I feel my throat constricting.

He drains his beer and places the bottle carefully on the table. He waves away my offer of another. "He told me about his job. About losing it, at least."

"Did he say why?" He nods. A memory flares. I remember the dark glee I felt when Hannah told me. "That's more than he ever admitted to me or mum."

"They had him bang to rights, he said. There was another guy involved, the boss's son, and he got off lightly, but that wasn't the point. He was greedy. A fool. Patrick's words."

"It was a tipping point. He was never exactly stable, but things got worse after that. For Hannah especially."

"He couldn't stand getting caught. He missed the money and the status but it was the … humiliation that he really hated. He lost it and he took it out on Hannah."

"He certainly did." He started to speak again. I stop him. "It's okay, Richard. Thanks, but I know all this. I don't need to hear it again."

"I think he's really sorry, Nick."

"I think he probably is. I'm just not sure what difference it makes."

"I think he'd agree. It's not forgiveness he's after; at least, I don't think it is."

"What then?"

"I think he's sick. He's lost weight, even since before Christmas, and he has this awful, hacking cough."

"He's a big boy. I'm sure he can find a doctor."

"That's what I told him, I even nagged him a little. The thing is, we were meant to meet up a couple of days ago and he didn't show."

"That's not a massive deal, not with Patrick."

"I've tried calling, but the line is dead."

"Perhaps he's changed his phone."

"Perhaps. But some of the things he said, Nick." He sits forward, his hands in his lap. "He told me he catches a bus to the coast some weekends, goes for long walks on the beach at Hunstanton. If it all gets too much, he said, he can just walk into the sea."

"That's Patrick's idea of a joke."

"I thought that, but now I'm not so sure. I think it *has* all got too much. I really do."

"No way," I say. "Not Patrick. He hasn't got it in him."

But even as I speak I wonder if it's true.

Chapter 17

They asked me to lunch one Sunday, a couple of weeks after they returned from their honeymoon. They asked mum too but she said she had a migraine.

Patrick relished playing the bountiful host, showing off his wife and home, rubbing it in. He spent some time explaining the vintage of a bottle of expensive wine that he opened as Hannah served the roast beef. I didn't understand a word, didn't care, the food was good and the drink was plentiful, that was enough for me. Hannah helped; she was pretty and warm and engaged and seemed to listen to what I said. She even flirted a little. Patrick didn't seem to mind. It even amused him, I think. I'd had girlfriends since I'd split up with Jessica but not many, and the gap between them was growing. I felt heady with the wine and Hannah's proximity.

He insisted on showing me his company car. It looked nice enough, but I don't even remember the make. I had no interest in cars, as Patrick well knew. He showed me his company credit card as well, brandishing it over dessert. "Expense account, little brother," he said, as though I was meant to be impressed. I caught something in Hannah's expression then, but I wasn't sure what it was.

Patrick worked as a loss adjuster for a national firm. He'd been in insurance for years, starting in sales and working his way up. I had no idea what his job entailed and didn't really care. He seemed to think it afforded him a certain status and perhaps it did. It was clearly important to him and, presumably, to Hannah as well.

"How's your work, Nick?" Patrick said. He was opening a second bottle of wine. Hannah was serving me another helping of trifle.

"Great," I said.

Hannah slid my bowl in front of me. I caught a hint of her perfume. "That doesn't sound very convincing."

"He's gone to work for his little school friend," Patrick said. "I told him, years ago; stay on at school, go to Uni, if you can find one that'll have you. But no, he knows best."

He was talking directly to Hannah. "I'm sitting right here," I said.

He looked straight at me. "Richard, right? Richard Butler? I remember him from school. Weaselly little sod. I had to give him a slap once for smoking pot in your room."

"Jesus," I said. Hannah took a long sip of wine. "He's not so bad," I said to Hannah. "His dad owns a couple of newsagents. I help out behind the counter and in the office sometimes. Accounts, stuff like that."

"You did Business Studies at sixth form, didn't you?"

I was astounded and flattered that she remembered. "Yeah. There was an accountancy module. I quite liked that."

"You quit after a year," Patrick said. "You couldn't have liked it that much."

I felt myself flush. Richard and I had both quit after a year. The truth is we messed around too much, got too far behind. He said we should try Norwich

Union, earn some money. Getting a job there was easy enough, but we both hated it. Richard moved onto the Stationary Office, which he loathed even more while I stuck with Norwich Union for a couple of years before getting a job in retail. Turns out dealing with the public was not for me, which wasn't much of a surprise. Richard's dad reluctantly gave his son a job and then, after I'd had a couple months of unemployment, Richard got me to join him.

"University isn't for everyone," Hannah said. "Look at Jessica."

"She got her degree," I said.

"I just hope it was worth it." We both looked at her. "She had a breakdown. I was backwards and forwards to Nottingham every couple of weeks during her first year. Mum and Dad ... well, it was difficult."

"She's never mentioned it," I said.

"I don't suppose she would," Hannah said. Her wine glass was full again and she held the stem in both hands. Colour was blooming in her cheeks. I thought of what Jessica had said, about their parents and about Hannah's denial.

"Anyway, Mum was pleased," I said.

"About what?"

Patrick broke in. "Nick quitting school, not going to University. She doesn't like us getting ideas above our station. Does she, Nick?"

I ate my trifle. "This is great," I said to Hannah. Hannah smiled and drank some wine.

"I'll be travelling a lot. For work," Patrick said later. Hannah started to clear the dinner things. I'd said I'd help, but she shooed me away.

"Poor Hannah." He caught the inflection in my voice and I felt his eyes on my face.

"I'll be brave," Hannah said.

"Take the piss, why don't you?" Patrick's face darkened.

I recognised the signs. "I'm joking," I said quickly. "I assume that's why you've got the car, the credit card. Pretty sweet."

"Yeah," he said slowly, "I suppose." The drink was on him now. Things could go either way.

"Anyway," Hannah said brightly, "I won't be lonely. I've got Nick."

"I'm sorry?" I said.

"You can manage the odd coffee or lunch, I hope? You won't leave your poor old sister-in-law to languish on her own?"

I sat up a little, watching Patrick's face. His expression went blank and then a smile formed and he laughed. "Yeah, Nick? Do you think you can spare the time? Between all those women of yours?"

I was happy to be patronised if it meant Patrick was back from the brink. "Maybe. I'll see what I can do. Mind you, how busy you teachers are, I doubt you'll have the time."

"With all those holidays we have, I'm sure I can squeeze a coffee in."

We were all smiling now and the atmosphere had an air of jollity that felt forced and brittle. I didn't like it much.

Hannah said she was going to wash up. Again I'd said I'd help and this time she didn't demur. Patrick shot me a look of bemused contempt. "I'm going for a walk," he said. Then to Hannah, "Put some coffee on? I've got a decent single malt to open when I get back."

In the kitchen Hannah threw me a tea towel and I caught it. "I hope I'm not stepping on Patrick's toes. Taking his job."

She snorted. "Seriously? The kitchen is *not* his domain. I suspect you know that."

"It's not a surprise. Let's leave it at that."

"No big deal. I don't need him lumbering around in here. I like it like this."

"Fair enough."

She gave me a sideways glance. "Hey, are you judging me?"

"It's not *you* I'm judging."

"Jesus, you two."

"Aren't we just delightful?"

She chuckled at that.

When Patrick returned we drank coffee and his good whisky. When it was time for me to go Hannah gave me a hug and made herself scarce.

Patrick said that he was too pissed to drive me home and offered to pay for a taxi. I said I'd walk. He said it was a long way and I told him it was fine. He called me a stubborn bastard and shoved a twenty pound note in my jacket pocket. I wanted to retrieve it and throw it at him, but I didn't. I thanked him for lunch and he grunted and I left.

It *was* a long walk home. I was tired and mostly sober at the end of it. I could still feel Hannah's hug though, the contours of her body against mine.

Chapter 18

The day after Richard's visit I walk into the city centre. The wind of the previous evening has died away and the day is still and cold. The light is pristine, the roads and pavements rimed with frost. My footsteps squeak as I walk. It takes about twenty minutes to reach the Millennium Library, which sits at the edge of the City's main shopping area.

I wander amongst the general fiction for a while. It feels good to be out of the cold. I select a few paperbacks, pretty much at random. I try reading the blurbs, but I can't really take anything in. I'm thinking of Patrick, of course, although I really don't want to. I tried calling him after Richard left and again before breakfast that morning, but the line was dead, as Richard said it would be.

I check out my books and order a drink at the coffee shop that abuts the library. The place is almost empty so I take my large hot chocolate to one of the comfortable armchairs that ring the café's perimeter. I settle down and pull out my phone and do something else I don't want to do.

My mother answers after three rings. "What do you want?"

We haven't spoken since Christmas Day. Her voice jars. "Have you spoken to Patrick?"

Her words are slow and carefully spaced out. "I haven't seen or heard from either of you since you abandoned me. You left me all alone on Christ …"

I hang up. I stare at the phone as though it's toxic. She rings back and I answer reluctantly.

"What's happened to Patrick?"

"Nothing's happened to Patrick. I just wondered, that's all."

"You're lying. I can hear it in …"

"I'll hang up again. And this time I won't answer when you call back."

There's a short, resentful silence. "You've worried me."

"I didn't mean to do that. Have you tried to contact him?"

"It's not my job to …"

"So that's a no. Okay. You don't need to worry. I'll let you know when I've spoken to him."

She starts to say something else, but I cut her off. Then I set the phone to silent and bury it deep in one of my coat pockets.

When I finish my drink I leave the warmth of the café and walk past St Peter Mancroft. I consider entering, taking a seat at one of the pews and settling myself in the stone cold, in the hushed silence, and praying to a God in whom I do not believe. A character in a book I enjoyed had a habit of tithing; he donated ten per cent of his earnings to the nearest church in his vicinity. I imagine taking a tenth of my cash and stuffing it in St Peter Mancroft's collection box. I pause for a moment outside the too-modern glass doors, then continue walking. I pass the trees that fringe the church's entrance. Their bare branches are embroidered with a soft, lingering mist.

The light is becoming muted, sepulchral, although it is not yet noon. I wander around the city centre for a while, passing precisely five bookmakers. Their doors are open, their walls made of glass. Maybe they beckon me, maybe they don't, but I'm tempted, of course. I keep walking, grimly, hands stuffed deep in pockets, head down, walking and walking.

When I stop its midday and I'm outside Jarrold's department store. I pull out my phone and call Jessica.

She answers quickly. "Nick?"

"I owe you lunch."

"Serendipity," she says.

"What?"

"Hannah is driving me fucking mental."

"I thought you could handle her?"

"I can … I mean … oh, piss off, Nick." I listen to the sound of her breathing. "Where are you?" I tell her. "Give me twenty," she says, and rings off.

We eat lunch at Jarrold's, in the salad bar on the third floor. Jessica has a large glass of white wine. "As you're paying." Her salad contains pears and walnuts and a blue cheese dressing. Mine is mostly ham and lettuce and a couple of tiny new potatoes. I pick at it listlessly.

"Eat up," she says. "Growing lad and all that."

"I'm not really feeling it."

"You're losing weight, Nick." It's almost as though she cares. My eyes feel hot suddenly and I blink a couple of times. "Are you okay?"

"I'm fine."

"You've had a shave, at least. Good boy."

"Good boy?"

"It takes years off you." She reaches a hand across and rubs my cheek. "Smooth as a baby's bum."

"Jessica. Jesus."

She sits back and sighs. "Oh, let me have my fun. I'm living with Hannah, for Christ's sake."

"I thought you were fine? That's what you said. At my flat."

She looks irritated. "I *was* fine, but now I'm not. That's kind of life, isn't it?"

"Is it that bad?"

"With Hannah? Yeah, it's bad. It's Steve this, Steve that; it's all I bloody hear about."

"I don't really want to ..."

"I mean, I've met him. He's a gammony *twat*." She's become animated. The room is sparsely populated but a couple of heads turn our way. She breathes out slowly. "Sorry."

"No problem. I'm surprised she'd go for ... that type."

"It's all the same to Hannah. It's a new host, isn't it? That's what matters."

"A new host?"

"Yeah. It's what she does, isn't it? It's not even her fault, not really. What are you looking like that for? I assumed you knew. You said as much, didn't you?"

"I did?"

"To Hannah? Something about you being her bridge back to normal people?"

"She told you that?"

"She tells me everything. Sisters, right?" She makes a mock gagging noise. "Anyhow; bull's-eye with that one, partner."

"Bulls-eye?"

"You got her bang to rights. She was impressed, actually; she didn't think you had it in you."

"I'm so immensely flattered." I can't hide the sarcasm.

"Nick?" She gives her empty wine glass an accusing glance. "Maybe I shouldn't have had this, not on an empty stomach. Such a *fucking* lightweight."

"It's fine."

"No. You're sulking. But … it's ancient history, is what it is." She eats some rocket and walnut and a tiny piece of pear. "Get me another glass of wine, why don't you?"

"Are you driving?"

"What are you my dad now? Gimme, gimme, Nick."

I fetch her a glass of wine and when I get back to the table she's propped forward with her face between her hands. "Sorry, mate."

"What for?"

"That took an odd turn."

"It's fine."

"So you said. Such silly words." She slips into an odd, mimicky voice. "It's okay. No problem. Don't worry about it." She shakes her head. "Such bullshit."

"Seriously, I'm …"

Her eyes meet mine and they are bright and wide and challenging. "We fucked once, right?"

That pulls me up short. I'd thought about it, of course, our history, in the days since her visit; the way her mouth tasted, the feel of her skin against mine. "More than once."

"I've had your cock in my mouth, Nick. I remember how you felt inside me." I feel myself flush. I start to say something, but she places a finger on my lips. "So we can cut the crap, can't we? We can do that, at least? For old times' sake?"

When I speak my voice is oddly bright and forced. "Of course."

"Good. So … how do you feel?"

I drink some water and feel something collapse inside me. "Hurt."

"By Hannah?"

"By what you said about Hannah. It's stupid, I know ..."

"I think it's human. Probably."

"Probably. But I've got no right to feel hurt." I take a breath and tell her about the second mortgage and how I'd forged Hannah's signature.

"Yeah," she says. "I know. Not cool."

"You know?"

"She's a talker, is Hannah. Mind you, I was astonished she ever put you on the mortgage in the first place."

"Her idea, actually. Not long after I moved in. It surprised me too."

"And I know about the girl. Tash, was it?"

"Of course you do."

"You were naughty, Hannah was naughty."

"But the money ... I mean, I'll pay her back ..."

"Of course you will. I wouldn't sweat it. Steve's loaded. He's a barrister, earns a gazillion pounds an hour. He's got one of those big houses on the Newmarket Road. He had a wife and a couple of kids as well, until Hannah came along."

"I'm going to pay her back. Somehow or other."

"Okay. I believe you. I think you'll try, at least."

I nod slowly and look at my hands. "Anyway," I say eventually. "How are you?"

She takes a long draught of wine. "Oh, I'm fucked, mate." Her smile is wide and off centre and just the tiniest bit manic. "I'm in the belly of the beast." She puts her glass down and her smile shrinks to normal size and becomes wry and self-deprecating. "Well, I'm living with Hannah, which is much the same thing."

"I'm sorry."

"I need a job. I need to get my own place."

"You could temp, maybe?"

She tilts her head. "Maybe."

I nudge a potato to the side of my plate. "You could come and stay with me for a bit."

"What?"

"Just as a stop gap; so you and Hannah don't end up killing each other. It'd be a bit cosy, but I could sleep on the sofa."

"Huh."

"Just a thought."

"A thought." She pushes her plate to one side. "Okay. Thanks, Nick."

"No problem. You'll think about it?"

"I'll think about it."

"Good. There is something else."

"Of course there is."

"Can I borrow your car?"

"My car?" She drains her wine and places the glass back on the table. "What do you need with my car?"

I tell her about Patrick.

I expect her to be dismissive, but she listens carefully and when I'm finished she says, "I can see why you're thinking what you're thinking."

"I thought you'd tell me I'm being silly." Perhaps I'd hoped that she would.

"It doesn't sound like Patrick. not that I knew him very well, or wanted to, but it doesn't fit with the Patrick that you describe. Or Hannah for that matter."

"Will you tell Hannah?"

"There's no point. She won't care." She sees the look on my face. "She just won't."

"I know; can't really blame her."

"How much do you care, Nick? Really?"

"He's sick, I think. And broken."

"He used to hit you, didn't he? Hannah said."

"Is there anything she hasn't told you?"

"Sisters," she says and shrugs.

"Yeah, he hit me. But he was damaged too." I think of something Richard said. "He could be kind as well, believe it or not. No-one is all bad."

"I'll take your word for it," Jessica says. "So, what's the plan, Stan?"

"Thought I'd take a trip out to his freezing shithole of a cottage, have a look around. Maybe visit that club, ask some questions."

"Detective Nick."

"Something like that."

"You could always go to the police."

"With what? He's an adult, after all."

"Or a close approximation, at least."

"If I don't get anywhere, don't find anything, then I'll report it."

"I bet your mum is freaking out."

"Probably. I need something to tell her as well. So is it okay? To borrow the car?"

"We can go together."

"Really?"

"Why not? How about this weekend? It'll get me out of the house, at least."

"That'd be great. Thanks, Jessica."

"No problem," she says.

We leave the store together and linger for a while on the pavement outside and then we say our goodbyes. She heads off towards St Andrew's Hall. I watch her until she disappears from view, then make my way back to my empty flat.

Chapter 19

It was several months before Hannah and I met up on our own. I hadn't taken her pronouncements over Sunday lunch particularly seriously and I'd completely forgotten about them when I got a text from her out of the blue late one summer afternoon.

Holiday's ending and I'm blue. Fancy a coffee with a lonely old cow? I'll pay.

My instinct was to reply straightaway, but I resisted. I did feel a thrill, though, sad bastard that I was. I didn't get much time to enjoy it, as guilt kicked in along with thoughts of Patrick. I'd seen them both a few times over the months, mostly at mum's. And we'd been out for a disastrous double date in the spring; my partner was a shy, pretty nurse called Leanne. She was far too good for me. I'm sure she would have realised this sooner or later, but that evening can only have served to clarify matters. Patrick was drunken and boorish. Over coffees and liqueurs he started running down the NHS. I'm not sure what his point was or even if he really had one. Perhaps he thought he was being funny. When I asked him about it later he said he couldn't remember anything. Hannah tried to stand up to him. I didn't. Leanne fought her corner well and I saw her continually glancing at me, expecting support. I didn't say anything much. Patrick frightened me sometimes. Often. I tried to explain this to her later but she wasn't interested. I didn't blame her.

I was gambling then. Not much, but enough. If I wasn't an addict then I was well on the way. I liked the numbness it brought, the way it melted an afternoon away. I'd met Ray by then; I didn't always use the Ladbrokes on Unthank Road, but I usually did. I liked Ray; he was dry and laconic and he seemed to hate his job. He'd counsel me sometimes in a gentle, offhand manner. Had I had enough, he'd say, after another loser, moustache bristling, eyes kind and querulous. He wasn't patronising, not quite, and, although I often ignored him, I indulged him too and it became a kind of joke between us. To me, at least.

I was at work when I got Hannah's text; I was in the office above Richard's dad's newsagents on Lincoln Street, messing around with an Excel spreadsheet. I was on my own, which suited me fine. Sometimes Richard would join me but he had become moody and sullen, resentful of his father and the control he had over him. He had plans, he said, bigger plans than this. He never said what they were.

I replied to Hannah eventually, trying to sound as casual and offhand as I could. Which wasn't saying much.

We met in a *Starbucks* in the city centre. It was just after lunch and the place was emptying out. The day was hot and Hannah wore a halter top and shorts and had her hair pulled back in a ponytail.

I tried to hide my excitement and my attraction. She gave me hug, which didn't help. I got us both iced coffees and we went upstairs and sat in leather armchairs across a small table, next to an upright fan that jittered noisily back and forth.

"Thanks for this," she said.

"My pleasure," I said, for once telling the unadulterated truth.

"I do have friends," she said suddenly. She sipped her drink. "I'm not really lonely."

"I didn't think you were."

"It's just, they're all teachers." She rolled her eyes. "Only so much talking shop a girl can take."

"Patrick away?"

"Lake District. It was Edinburgh last week."

"Must be hard."

"Must it?" she said, through a half-smile. "If you say so."

I sat forward awkwardly. "Look, does Patrick know ..." I faltered.

"That I'm here? With you? Of course he does." Now she leant forward and I could see the top of her breasts. "What," she said, taunting. "Do you think this is a date?"

"No. God, no, of course not. I just wondered ..."

She smiled and her teeth were very white. "I'm only teasing, Nick. Don't mind me."

"It's fine."

"You probably get enough of that from Patrick, don't you?"

"Honestly, I'm fine." I felt the heat in my face. I suddenly wished that I wasn't there at all.

"I'm sorry," she said. "Look, let's start again." She reached out a hand and I took it. It was firm and cool. "Hi. I'm Hannah."

"Nick," I said.

"Great. Now be a sweetheart and go and get me a shortbread, I'm starving."

I did as I was told.

We sat there for almost two hours. She was easy company; warm, interested. We touched on family matters, but only briefly and we deftly avoided anything spiky or difficult. She was a maths teacher and she talked about that for a bit; the grind of it, the endless cuts and curriculum changes. That led us to politics and we had a moan about the Tories and wondered where the hell they were leading us. Patrick wouldn't talk about that stuff, she said. He wasn't interested, he said, didn't care.

"Sounds like Patrick. Could be worse, I suppose. He could have turned out like mum."

"What do you mean?"

"You must have gathered? Her politics … let's just settle on bitter old reactionary, shall we?"

"I get the bitter bit, I've not noticed the other."

"Perhaps she doesn't lay it on too thick when you're around. She must really like you."

"Yeah, Nick, she *really* likes me."

"Who wouldn't?"

"So sweet," she said, although her eyes became distant.

"Does it matter? Patrick's politics?"

"Not really. Just curious. I'd like to think he wouldn't vote for this lot."

"I'm not sure he's ever voted at all. But, no, I don't think he would. Not that I'd go mistaking him for a woolly liberal, however."

"Well, no," she said.

A little later she glanced at her phone then gathered her bag and purse together. "This has been lovely, Nick. Thank you. We'll do it again?"

"Of course."

Another hug and a kiss this time; on the cheek, very faint, but still. Her scent was fresh and lemony. I smelt it on me later as I sat at the kitchen table with mum, eating beans on toast.

*

We did do it again, but not for a while and not that often, not at first at least. Hannah had school and I was working hard on my gambling addiction and trying to figure out how I could quietly steal some cash from Richard's father's business.

A year or so later Patrick took up golf. I found this amusing and ridiculous; he'd never shown the slightest interest in the sport before.

"Networking," he said curtly. "You wouldn't understand. It gives you and Hannah more time for your cosy little coffee mornings, though, doesn't it? So I guess we're all happy."

"Delirious," I said.

But, he was right, it did, and Hannah and I started meeting up every other weekend or so. The coffees melded into walks and lunches and trips to the cinema. We saw *Calvary* and *The Grand Budapest Hotel* and *Mr Turner*. She liked them all, she said, although only *Calvary* really did it for me.

One Sunday Patrick's golf was called off at the last minute and he joined us at Cinema City and we watched *Chef* together. It was exquisitely awkward; for me, at least, and I sensed for Hannah also.

Later, at the bar, with Hannah in the bathroom, he said, "Crap film."

"I liked it."

"You would." He passed me my pint. "Thanks, though."

"What for?"

"Looking after the little lady when I'm away."

"Little lady?"

He shrugged.

*

The next time Hannah and I met up on our own we ate scones and drank tea in a quaint café in a village near the Broads.

"It didn't work, did it?" Hannah said, wiping clotted cream from the corner of her mouth. "Last time. The three of us."

"I hated it."

"Actually, I did too."

We were both quiet for a while. It was early spring and we were emerging from a drab, attritional winter. The café was bustling and tentative sunlight eased in through the open door and the large picture windows.

"I'm not sure that this is right," she said eventually. She was working scone-crumbs around her plate with her forefinger. "Us. Meeting like this. I don't think it's working."

Something dropped in my stomach. "I don't see why not." My voice had a thin, wheedling quality that I didn't like at all.

"Nick."

"Patrick doesn't mind. He even thanked me."

"Thanked you?"

I did a terrible Patrick impersonation. "For looking after the little lady."

It earned a smile that it didn't deserve. "Sounds like Patrick. Well, not the voice, but ..."

"I know what you mean."

"The thing is ... Patrick's jealous."

"Not of me."

"No," she said gently. "Not of you."

Of course not. I was no threat. Letting me spend time with Hannah was just rubbing it in. "Look at what you could have won," I said.

"What?"

"Nothing. Mind doodles. Nothing at all. You were saying?"

Her expression, which had gone blank, came back into focus. "He's jealous, Nick. Of other men. Not that there *are* other men." That made me wonder and I briefly felt a stab of jealousy of my own. "He checks my phone, asks me about the other staff. He can't *stand* parent-teacher evenings."

"I'm sorry." I wished I could say I was surprised, but I couldn't.

"It's not your fault."

"Not sure what it's got to do with this, though. You said he's not jealous of me."

She went to pour herself some more tea but the pot was empty. I said I'd get some hot water but she told me not to bother. "I can handle Patrick. I'm not saying it's always easy, but ... I can handle him." She reached a hand out and touched mine briefly. "It's the pair of you. Coming between you, *that* I can't handle."

"There's nothing to come between."

"That's not true, is it, Nick? There's *something*. I mean it's as toxic as hell, but there's something."

"It wouldn't bother me if I never saw my brother again."

"I don't believe that. And it isn't the point."

"What is the point?"

"Your family; it's just a massive fucking void, isn't it?" Her voice had become louder and a couple at an adjacent table glanced at us in irritation.

I thought of her family then and of the lies they kept; walls of denial, built wide and deep. My voice went flat. "It's no big deal. Patrick's a bully. It's not as though he hides it. He used to hit me. He scares me. I'm not proud of it, but there it is."

"He used to hit you?"

"I thought you knew."

"How would I know?"

I thought everyone knew. I thought it was written all over me. "It was years ago. And it wasn't just me. It wasn't all the time, though, and it wasn't that hard, not really."

"Jesus."

"It was mostly on mum's behalf; I always kind of saw him as her henchman. And, to be fair, I was a stroppy little bastard."

"That's no excuse."

"Perhaps it is. It's no big deal. Different times and all that. And Hannah? Not a word. Please?"

"My lips are sealed."

"Thanks."

The silence that followed could have been awkward, but it wasn't.

So our meetings continued and nothing seemed to change much until one Sunday morning a year later when we were walking in Earlham Park. She'd seemed quiet and a bit off and when I asked her about it she stopped and turned to me and put a hand on my arm. "Nick," she said. "Something's happened."

Chapter 20

Jessica picks me up on Saturday morning and I squeeze into the passenger seat of her little Micra. She has the heating on high, even though the weather has relented a little and the day is milder, with a stiff, irregular breeze. Banks of cloud gather and ungather in the east.

I unzip my jacket. "I really appreciate this."

"So you said. Look, I'm sorry about the other day. I was a bit … hyper. I was late taking my meds."

"That's what I love about you, Jessica. You get straight to it."

"It's what we said, isn't it? No bullshit."

"I suppose. But, a little chat about the weather, about what's on TV? It wouldn't hurt, would it?"

She makes a little grunting noise and looks straight ahead, hands on the steering wheel, the engine still idling. "It's cold and windy. I quite like the new series of *Shetland*. Happy now?"

I slip my seat belt on. "Absolutely. What was that about meds?"

"I'm fine if I take them. If I don't, not so much."

"What are they for?"

She fiddles with the heater. "Jesus, it's boiling in here." She unbuttons her coat and throws her scarf onto the back seat. She wears a bottle-green roll-neck underneath the coat. She's painted her nails and she has some make up on, just enough. Her dark hair falls in artful bangs across her forehead. She's made an effort: for me, presumably.

"You don't have to tell me. Not my business."

She sighs. "It was me that said no bullshit."

"Still ..."

"I'm bipolar."

"I'm sorry."

She shrugs. "No biggie. The drugs *do* work. As long as I take them. And I nearly always take them."

I remember something that Hannah had said, years ago. "Did you have a breakdown? At uni?"

"How did ... Hannah, I assume?"

"This is going back some. After you and I split up, when she was with Patrick. She said something about seeing you through it, visiting you at Nottingham."

"Well, that's all crap. I saw myself through it. Somehow. She never came to Nottingham, not that I'd have wanted her to. Neither her nor mum and dad have ever acknowledged that I was ill at all."

"Jesus."

"It's possible that she believes that she helped me, played the dutiful big sister. It's hard to tell, with Hannah." I think of something that Richard had once said; about all our separate realities and how they overlap. "Deep shit, huh? And we're still sitting outside your flat. Shall I put the radio on?"

"Please."

She fiddles with the tuner until she finds Radio One. "Don't judge me," she says, slipping the car into gear and pulling out into the empty street.

It's late morning by the time we reach Patrick's house. Jessica parks opposite the cottage and sits with the engine idling. "Why on earth did he move here?"

We look across at the sweep of dun-coloured fields and meadows that surround the cluster of houses. Clouds scud past, hugging close to the flat land.

The bleakness and sense of isolation is tangible. "Perhaps it looks better in summer."

"Perhaps."

"I don't know, is the honest answer. After Hannah he lived with mum for ages. It's an antidote to that maybe. He's away from Norwich, I suppose; all those memories."

"He's away from everything."

"I think it's a penance. He's living in a freezing shithole, he has no car, he has to get the bus to work. Richard said he sleeps at the club sometimes, when he can't get a lift back. On the office floor."

"Penance? What good is that to anyone? Sounds more like self-pity to me."

"Probably. It's hard to tell with Patrick."

She turns the ignition off. "Why are we here, Nick?"

I shrugged. "I don't know. I've got to do something."

"Why? You don't owe him anything."

"He's my brother. What would you do? If it was Hannah?"

She exhales extravagantly. I'm aware of her scent and of her proximity. "I suppose I'd try and find the bitch."

"Well, there we go, then." I undo my seatbelt and open the door. A sliver of chilled air forces its way in. It's colder here in the fens. "Shall we?"

Jessica doesn't move. "Close the door a minute, Nick." I do as I'm told. She hesitates for a moment and something twists in the pit of my stomach. "Look, it's been nice. Seeing you again." She turns to face me. Her prettiness seems amplified in the confines of the car. "I think you may be becoming a bit less of a prick."

"Thanks. Means a lot. I sense there's a 'but' coming."

"There's always a but. Terms and conditions, shit like that."

"I thought we were cutting the crap? All I can hear are riddles ..."

"We're not going to shag, is what I'm trying to say."

"Okay."

"Just to get it out there. Clear the air."

"I haven't even said anything ..."

"Come on, Nick. You're a man, after all."

"Well, that's offensive."

"Are you telling me you haven't thought about it?"

Of course I have. "I'm certainly thinking about it now."

"So am I."

"You are?"

She turns back to face the window and stares out at Patrick's cottage. "I'm in the prime of my life. Apparently. According to *Cosmo*. And I don't like being alone. I don't *hate* it, not like Hannah. Jesus, *nothing* like Hannah. But ... it would be easy, wouldn't it? We know each other that way. It'd be like slipping on an old coat."

"That's so romantic."

"The thing is ... I'm seeing someone."

"Ah."

"Not like that. She's a counsellor or a therapist or whatever the fuck it is she calls herself. I'm working through some issues."

"How's that going?"

"She's lovely; warm and engaging. But she keeps asking these questions that I really don't want to answer and by the end of our hour together I just want to punch her in the face."

"Sounds great."

"It's a process. Thing is, I don't want to muddy the

waters. My waters are quite muddy enough as it is. A friend would be good, though? If that's okay?"

"I'll do my best, what with my raging libido and all." She smiles at that and touches my arm. "I suppose that means you moving in is out of the question?"

"I dunno. We've had this chat. I'm back on my meds. We're both adults. Kind of. I'll see what Tabitha says."

"Tabitha?"

"Yeah. I know. But she's okay. I really like her when I don't want to kill her."

I open my door again. "No worries, let me know when you know."

"So sweet," she says. She opens her door as well and we step out into the day.

Chapter 21

We were on the slope that led down to the river. It was an early spring day, dull and featureless. There was a bench and we sat on it.

"Hannah? What's happened?"

"Patrick. He's lost his job."

I wasn't proud of the dark stab of glee that I felt, but it was there just the same. "What did he do?"

She turned towards me. The day was fine and dry and cool. Her eyes were colourless in the flat light. "Who said he did anything?"

"It's Patrick. He did something."

She braced herself, linked her hands together and placed them in her lap, and told me.

It turns out being a loss adjuster is more complicated than I realised. I think I did Patrick a disservice. I assumed that if it was a job that he could do well it must be especially simple and undemanding. As a lead adjuster with a firm used by all of the major insurance companies his responsibilities were wide and varied. He was handling claims that often involved settlements running well into six figures. Many parties were involved and their interests often conflicted. It was Patrick's job to bring them together, without too much conflict or loss of faith or funds.

He was also responsible for appointing the contractors needed to carry out remedial works to buildings or business premises that had suffered often catastrophic damage after fire or flood or any other unfortunate, unforeseen event. The contracts involved were large and it was no surprise or secret that the companies in question cultivated close working relationships with adjuster's like Patrick. Golf days, expensive meals, little gifts; all declared, everything above board, part of the grease that oiled the corporate world's myriad, endless wheels.

What wasn't part of it – or it shouldn't have been, at least – was taking backhanders from a small but select coterie of builders and roofers and shop-fitters to ensure that their tenders won the day, more often than not. That was not acceptable. Nor was getting caught.

"They did an audit, I assume?" I said finally, after she'd sat back and taken a breath.

"Of course they did. Patrick said that he was careful, that they couldn't have known. He thinks someone grassed him up."

"Sure he does. It can't be his fault, can it?"

Her fingers twisted in her lap. "I don't understand. It's not as though we need the money."

"It'll never be enough, not for Patrick." She stood and so I did. Skirting the riverbank, we walked eastward, towards the UEA. "Are they pressing charges?"

"They're hushing it up. I mean, he had to pack his desk up, there and then, and he was escorted off the premises. But he'll get a reference if he doesn't make a fuss. They don't need any scandals. Mustn't scare the shareholders."

"I doubt he's the only one."

"He says he isn't. The thing is, he hit someone."

"Of course he did."

"As they were seeing him out of the office he broke away and pinned this guy in the corner; called him a prick and punched him in the face. It took three of them to pull him away. It was the boss's son."

"Fuck's sake, Patrick." She stopped walking suddenly and stood facing the river. The water was very low. "Are you all right?"

"No." Her voice had become small. "I want a hug."

"Okay." It was brief and very gentle. I savoured it though. I smelled her scent. She had a little more perfume on that day, I noticed, and a bit more make up too.

"Thank you." She pulled away and we walked again. "Sorry. I'm being silly."

"Not at all."

"We'll be okay. For money, at least for a while."

"How much did he ..." I struggled to find the correct word.

"I don't know. He wouldn't tell me. And it's all gone, he says."

"Do you believe him?"

"No," she said bluntly. "I don't. He says he'll find another job, when he's ready, but he's done with insurance. He's acting as though he's been wronged, Nick. As though he's a martyr. And he's so *angry*."

"Well, this is Patrick we're talking about."

"And he's drinking."

"Patrick's always drinking."

"Not like this. Oh shit," she said, and I saw that she was close to tears. I reached for her arm but she shrugged me away.

"You should leave him," I said.

Her laugh was the briefest thing. "Right."

"You could."

"Stop it, Nick," she said. We walked back towards the car.

As she pulled her seat belt across her chest and slid the key into the ignition, she said, "I've been sworn to secrecy, by the way. You haven't heard this from me. He's going to tell you and mum in his own time. And in his own way."

"Can't wait."

"And ... he doesn't know about this. Our meeting up. Not this time. I didn't tell him."

"Okay," I said, and the tiniest thrill, the merest bubble of excitement formed in the pit of my stomach.

I was still living with mum at this time. I couldn't afford otherwise. As my gambling increased I managed to convince myself, with an addict's self-deception, that it was only a matter of time before I won enough to pay off my debts and finally move out of the family home. I was stealing from work. Not too much, I wasn't greedy, just enough to keep me ticking over. It occurred to me years later that if I'd simply put the money I stole aside and kept away from the horses, I would have been able to have moved out years ago. I never said I was a genius.

The house was big enough that we could keep out of each other's way most of the time, my mother and I. We still ate most of our meals together at the kitchen table, invariably in a chilly silence. Out of habit, I suppose. After we'd eaten I'd wash up as she stood outside the kitchen window and smoked angrily; three cigarettes a day, one after each meal. "You see, I can stop," she said once, hovering at the kitchen door. "Anytime. I'm not an addict." I don't know how she knew about the gambling, but, of course, she did. It was another example of my weakness, my moral lack. I was going to hell, she said once, casually, without heat, as I passed her in the living room. I didn't take it to heart; sometimes she believed in God, sometimes she didn't.

Another habit, long ingrained, was the serving of crab-paste rolls at teatime on a Saturday; white rolls, margarine, Shippam's crab paste. Cucumber occasionally, but not often. A pot of strong tea. Every Saturday, week after week, for years and years. I hated crab paste, but I ate it because I always had done.

The Saturday after I'd met Hannah at Earlham Park she and Patrick joined us. "What a treat," he said, barrelling into the kitchen, pulling up a chair and sitting with his elbows propped on the table. I searched his expression for irony. Hannah took a seat to my right. She asked how I was, Patrick didn't.

Mother joined us, her hand brushing Patrick's shoulder as she passed his chair. As she sat and poured us cups of creosote-coloured tea, he said loudly, "Great news. I've quit my job."

The pouring stopped. "Patrick?"

Hannah was pale and quiet. I put on my surprised face. I was a decent actor. You have to be in my family.

"Insurance," he said. His grin was too wide and way off centre. Faint red lines threaded across both of his eyes. "Twenty years is more than enough."

"But what will you do?" Our mother's voice had become small and plaintive. I think she'd enjoyed my brother's status, his company car and expense account, almost as much as he had.

"I've given them enough," he said. "Too much, really. I've got plans, don't you worry. Big plans."

"Care to share them?" I said.

"Not yet, little brother. All in good time." His eyes fixed on mine, but only briefly. "And another thing, I'm going to be a father."

"My goodness," our mother said, a bony hand snaking out and gripping Patrick's wrist. "How wonderful."

I was watching Hannah. Her eyes became wide open, her expression one of shock and horror. "I'm not pregnant," she said, her voice shrill and incredulous.

"What?" our mother said. "Oh."

"Not yet," Patrick said, patiently, as though speaking to a child. "It's just a matter of time."

"We haven't even talk …" Hannah started to say but Patrick cut her off.

"We're not getting any younger. And I don't want an only child."

"Jesus," someone said. It may have been me.

"How wonderful," our mother said again. "And about time. Do you hear this, Nicholas?"

"I'm not deaf."

Hannah stood. All eyes turned towards her. She was trembling and what colour there had been in her face had fled entirely. "I'd like to go now."

"We haven't even eaten," Patrick said.

"You've got to keep your strength up," my mother said.

"I'd like to go …"

"We're not going anywhere," Patrick said quietly. "Not yet."

Hannah sat, quite suddenly, as though she were a marionette and somebody had cut her strings.

I could have left, I suppose. God knows I wanted to. But I didn't want to abandon Hannah. She couldn't look at me, though, and she didn't speak to me at all.

*

When they had finished eating and Hannah had scuttled out of the back door, Patrick put a hand on my chest, fingers spread wide, and pushed me towards the living room.

"I think the meetings have got to stop, don't you?" he said. "It's all got a bit too cosy."

"I think that's up to Hannah."

He dug his fingers in. "You really think that, little brother. Don't you?"

I tried not to move back or to look away from his face. It was hard. I remembered that hand, the flat of it, at least, the feel of it against the side of my head. But his eyes did not match the cold anger that was stitched on his face; I thought I saw something lost there, something scared. "What is wrong with you?"

"There's nothing wrong with me." His hand dropped.

"Look, if you ever need to talk …"

He shoved me hard in the chest and I staggered back against an armchair. "Fuck off."

He left, pushing past our mother, who stood to one side, watching impassively.

Chapter 22

We pause before approaching Patrick's house. The curtains are open but there is no obvious sign of life. The frontage is exposed red brick, the same as the rest of the terrace. The pointing is shabby, even from a distance. The window frames have faded to an off-cream and the paint is peeling.

"I've got a bad feeling about this," I say.

Jessica comes to my side and her shoulder nuzzles mine. "I'm sure he's fine. I doubt he'll be pleased to see you though."

"Do you think he's here?"

"Only one way to find out. Stop putting it off."

We approach the front door together and I knock and there's no answer. Traversing a crooked, shabby path we make our way to the back door. It's locked and I knock again to no avail. There's a pot containing a dead plant to the side of the door. I check underneath it, but there's no key. "That always works on TV."

Jessica is looking in through the kitchen window. "No sign of intelligent life. Which isn't to say that Patrick's not here, of course." I give her a look. "What?"

I shout his name a couple of times. All I get back is a chilly echo. "I'm not sure I've thought this through."

"We could break in." I give her another look. "It'd be easy enough. All this glass. Plenty of stones in this so-called garden."

"No point. He isn't here." I knew I was right. The house felt abandoned and even more desolate than when I'd visited before Christmas.

"There may be some clues inside."

"You mean like a suicide note?"

After a moment she says, "I don't mean that at all."

"I'm sorry. Let's try the front again. Perhaps he's hidden a key somewhere."

We walk down the side of the house. As we reach the front door we see a woman hovering by the gate. She's small and elderly with dyed black hair set in a fierce perm. Thin legs peek out of the bottom of a long, black, heavy coat. Her features are vague but her eyes are pin-sharp and they fix on us now as she leans against the wrought-iron gate. "Are you looking for Patrick?"

"Yes, I'm …"

"Are you bailiffs?"

"Why would we be bailiffs?" Jessica says.

"I miss Patrick." Her voice becomes querulous. "Where is he? Do you know where he is?" I start to say something, but she continues, "I have to do my own shopping now. And the buses … don't get me started on the buses. I can't get around like I used to, you see. Well, what would you know, at your age? Can't expect you to understand. But Patrick did. He was very good. A real people person. That's what I said to him, you should work with people, helping people, not in that grubby little club with all those gays." She points at the cottage next to Patrick's. "I live there. I've left the door open. Oh dear, the cold will be getting in." She looks towards us and her eyes are bright and shimmering. "My name's Ivy. Can I make you some tea? You look frozen, the pair of you."

*

Jessica and I sit next to each other on an ornate, over-stuffed sofa. We've both taken our coats off as the room is far too warm. It's neat and clean, but cluttered. An old-fashioned dresser dominates one wall; the surface is crammed with ornaments and candles and black and white photographs in heavy gilt frames. There's an air freshener plugged into a socket next to the sofa; the scent it releases is sweet and cloying and chemical-edged. There are other smells lurking beneath, I think, but I don't want to dwell on them. Jessica and I exchange a glance as we listen to Ivy bustling around in her kitchen. A kettle comes to the boil, teaspoons clink against china. "I'm eighty eight," she calls through. "Fifty years I've been here. Fifty years next summer. Thirty of them with Albert. Should have been more, of course, but … well, he was such a silly, stubborn man. It's cold out, I said. Wear a scarf, I said. And some gloves. Better still, stay here, with me, in the warm. Would he listen? Caught a chill. Of course he caught a chill, and that was that." She comes into the room, shouldering the door fully open. She's not entirely steady so I stand and take the tray from her and place it on the table in the centre of the room. "Thank you, dear." She still has her coat on despite the stultifying heat. She pours cups of weak tea and passes them across to us with shaking hands. "My best china, you are honoured." A tiny smile. "Ivy patterned, see? Albert bought me this set as an anniversary present. Ivy for Ivy, he said. He could be sweet when he wasn't being stubborn. He wasn't much to look at, but he was steady. That's the main thing, isn't it? Looks aren't everything, are they, dear?" This is directed at Jessica. Startled, she just has time to blurt out "no" before Ivy continues, "Have some biscuits." She pushes a plate of shortbread towards us. We both take a piece. "Good. Look at the pair of you, no meat on your bones. You need feeding up. Like Patrick; I said, you're too thin and getting thinner. I made him pies and stews and jam tarts. I'd take them round, leave them on the doorstep if he wasn't there. I don't know if ate them but he always brought the plates back, shiny as a new pin. He was good like that. He'd do my shopping sometimes as well, take a bus into King's Lynn specially. That was such a help, as I can't get around like I used to." She fumbles in a coat pocket and pulls out a crumpled sheet of lined paper. "I have a list. Are you going anywhere near the shops? Could you pick these up for me, it's only a few things?"

"I'm sure we can, Ivy," I say, taking the list. "When was the last time you saw Patrick?"

"The last time I saw Patrick? Well, let me think." She places her cup back down and tea slops into the saucer. "It was bin day, so it must have been a Tuesday. He'd usually put them out for me, but he didn't. I thought he'd forgotten. I had to put them out myself and it isn't easy, what with my arthritis and everything." She holds out her hands as though we've requested evidence; a tracery of blue veins, swollen knuckles, fingers bent in on themselves. "So that was Tuesday, two weeks ago and actually, I didn't see him then, because he didn't put my bins out, did he? It was the Sunday before. That's right." She gives a little sigh of satisfaction. "I made him lunch. He sat right there." She looks straight at me. "With the plate on his lap. He ate most of it. He was worried, he said. Couldn't pay the rent. He was worried he was going to have to leave me on my own. I told him I'd pay his rent, but he laughed it off. He wouldn't have any of it; too proud, too stubborn, just like my Albert and look where that got him." Her expression becomes opaque as her eyes turn downwards. "Where is he, do you think? What's become of him?"

"I'm sure he's fine, Ivy. Look …"

"And that awful cough. It went right through him. I heard him at night, sometimes. The walls are thin here, see. So I said to him, you … must … call … the … doctor. Would he listen? I gave him an old bottle of Tixylix, but that didn't do any good. I didn't know what to do. If I hadn't given Albert's coats to the Sally Army years ago he could have had them. Wrapped himself up a little. I don't feel the cold, that's what he said. I told him, that's rubbish. We *all* feel the cold, whether we know it or not. And then there was the drink, of course."

"The drink?"

"It was always on his breath. Didn't matter what time of day it was. I didn't say anything. He was kind to me and I didn't want to hurt his feelings. And who can blame him, with what he'd been through?"

"What do you mean?"

"Losing his mother like that. Murdered. Awful, awful …"

"He said his mother was murdered?" I'm leaning forward now and I feel Jessica's hand on my thigh, holding me back.

"In her bed. Intruders. They broke in and killed her in her bed." She closes her eyes and shudders. "Can you believe it? What is this country coming to? Albert always said it was going to the dogs and that was years and years ago and it isn't getting any better now, is it? Poor Patrick. It's why he came here, he said; to get away from the memories. And that poor woman. Younger than me, she was. I lay here on my own at night sometimes and I wonder what she was thinking, when she heard them break in, when she knew they were coming for her. I know she was German, but still, that doesn't mean …"

"German? What the …" Jessica gives my leg a squeeze as Ivy's stream of consciousness continues.

"Her parents, dear. German. Held here after the war. Not Nazi's, though. That's what Patrick said; not Nazi's, not really, but not *not* Nazi's, if you know what I mean. It was the times, wasn't it, dear? You did what you had to do and who are we to judge? That's what I said to Patrick. And it wasn't her fault, was it, his mother, what with her just a child. No judgement here, I said. Now, Albert ... well, I expect he would have judged, but he's long gone as we all know. And his father came back with a funny leg from Monte Cassino, so it's hard to blame him, really, isn't it?" I stand suddenly and a side plate falls to the floor and a shortbread biscuit with it. Ivy's eyes track upwards. "Is everything all right, dear? Is it the cramp? My Albert got the cramp and his father, but then he would, what with his leg and ..."

"No, Ivy. It's not cramp. I'm fine. I just need some air, that's all. You stay here in the warm, I won't be a moment."

Jessica follows me outside. The air is cold and there's a stiffening breeze. Our breath turns to smoke as we face each other. "Easy, Nick."

"It's all bullshit. Patrick's lost his mind." I realise I'm still holding Ivy's shopping list. "Can I borrow your car? I'll go and pick this shopping up. I need to clear my head."

"What am I going to do?"

"Stay with Ivy? See what else she has to say. For what it's worth."

"Okay. I suppose." She throws me her keys. "Just don't be too long."

I thank her and head for her car as she turns, reluctantly, back towards Ivy's house.

Chapter 23

The thing with gamblers is, sometimes they win.

I didn't usually bother with multiple bets; I'd usually plough through an afternoon a race at a time, betting on them individually with a dogged, hypnotic determination. Winners popped up here and there – law of averages and all that – not enough to buttress the losers, of course, not nearly enough, but sufficient to polish the patina of self-deception that every addict needs.

A day after that appalling Saturday teatime with Patrick and Hannah I buried myself in the Ladbrokes on Unthank Road. I needed to erase the memory of Hannah's white, shocked face and the thought that our meetings had, in all probability, ended. I like to think I spared a thought for her feelings, marooned with Patrick as she was, but I suspect it was me that I was worried about and me alone.

Ray said hi as I approached the counter. The top two buttons of his shirt hung open and his tie was wildly askew. I could see that he was about to produce a quip of some sort, as he usually did, but the expression on my face must have made him pause. "Everything all right, young man?"

"Just peachy."

He sniffed. "Have you been drinking?"

"Couple of pints."

"Drinking *and* gambling." He made a disapproving face. His eyes were smiling, though, as they usually were, to take the edge off.

"It can hardly make my judgement any worse." He tilted his head to acknowledge the point. "I'd like a cup of your finest tea and the *Racing Post*, please."

He provided both without further comment and I took them to one of the red plastic tables at the far end of the shop. The first race was ten minutes away and the place was growing busy. Alongside the usual blank betting slips was a selection of pre-printed coupons covering a variety of multiple bets.

A Canadian covers twenty-six bets across five races, in combinations of singles, doubles, trebles and so on. A couple of winners from the five selections would probably get you your money back, depending on the odds. Four or five winners ... well, that was mug punter dreamland. And bets like these were very much for mug punters, designed to suck them in and hoover up their money and leave them cursing their luck and fantasising about hitting a jackpot that was, surely, only another five races away.

I knew all this but I filled out the bet anyway. I did it quickly, without much thought or consideration.

"This is unlike you," Ray said, as I handed over the slip.

"Fancied a change; it's as good as a rest, apparently."

"So they say." He handed me my change. "But what do they know?"

"More than me, I reckon."

I took another cup of tea back to my table and slumped in the chair. I flicked through the *Racing Post* and then through various items on my phone. My mother had been especially unbearable since Patrick's outburst the evening before. The prospect of being a grandmother had rendered her giddy and almost hysterical.

"She's not even pregnant yet," I said.

"You heard Patrick; it's just a matter of time."

"I don't get why you care so much." I nearly added that she certainly didn't seem to relish being a mother, but I didn't.

"You wouldn't understand," she said, and she was right about that, at least.

The first horse won. I barely noticed as I was studying the form for a sprint handicap at Ascot and there were only five minutes between the two races. As I placed my bet for the Ascot race – which lost, obviously – Ray said, "You've got the first one up. Four pounds back guaranteed. Heady stuff."

"Take the piss, why don't you?"

"I will. Thanks." His moustache twitched as he spoke. "Actually, though, your second pick has got a decent chance. If your double comes in you may even get your money back."

"Be still my beating heart."

It won easily, as it turned out, and so did my third selection, albeit at relatively short odds. Still, some rudimentary maths confirmed that my winnings were approaching three figures with two horses still to come. I'd covered the losses from the single bets that I'd had that afternoon with a bit to spare.

I approached the counter again and Ray put his finger to his lips.

"What?"

"Do you want to broadcast this?" he said, his voice low. "If one of the others comes in we're talking a grand, maybe more."

"Thanks for the thought. I mean, it's not going to happen, but yeah, let's keep it between us."

"You never know," he said.

I smoothed my crumpled slip out on the counter in front of us and together we peered at the final two selections, both double-figure odds, both thoughtless, throwaway choices. "Yeah, I think we do."

Not for the first time, I was wrong.

It came down to the final two races of the day; one from Ascot, the other from Wolverhampton. Most of the other punters had drifted away and there were only three of us left; a young guy in a shell suit, who was banging away mindlessly on one of the fixed odds machines, and an older man that I didn't recognise. I sensed that he had an inkling that something was going on, but neither Ray nor I would meet his gaze and eventually he left, just before the penultimate race started.

It was a twenty-runner apprentice handicap, a nightmare of a betting medium. I don't know what I was thinking choosing a horse from that particular race. I don't suppose I was really thinking at all.

"It's got some course and distance form," Ray said as they were loading the stalls. Indeed it had, from a couple of years ago, but it hadn't even been placed in the current season.

"It's a shit horse in a shit race. I think I just liked the colours or something."

"You were a bit drunk."

"I had two pints, Ray."

As often happens in apprentice races, they went off too quickly. The favourite and a couple of other fancied runners wore themselves out in a desperate attempt to take an early lead. My selection had no choice but to sit off the pace as he wasn't quick enough to go with them, but as the final three furlongs approached and the leaders faltered, there was only going to be one winner.

"Bloody hell," Ray said.

The final furlong seemed to take an eternity as my horse scooted clear. It was eased down as the finish line approached and another outsider stayed on to within a couple of lengths. My buttocks clenched a little as the commentator's voice quickened in an attempt to drum up a sense of jeopardy, but the result was not really in doubt.

"Jesus Christ. Ray … how much …"

"Easy," he said. "Not yet. There's another race to go. We'll work it out then."

"It's 25-1, Ray. It's got no chance and I don't care. I just want to know …"

"Just wait. It's only a few minutes. Get some air or something."

"I don't want any air." I pulled a chair from under a nearby table and sat on it, but then stood again instantly and went back to the counter. The guy at the fixed odds machine suddenly lashed out at the terminal, kicking it hard, twice.

"Easy, mate," Ray said.

"Fuck off," the guy shouted, turning to face us. He was younger than I thought and looked close to tears. We all waited for a moment and I found that I was bracing myself. Then he kicked the machine again and aimed a final volley of abuse in our direction, before barrelling out into the street. The door swung slowly shut behind him.

Ray took a breath. "Quite a day," he said.

The final race was a sprint handicap on the all-weather at Wolverhampton. "And why did you choose this little beauty?" Ray asked.

The horses were circling at the start. I felt sick. "I liked the name."

"Apple Tree Yard. It has got a ring to it. It used to be quite decent."

"Back when the old king was alive."

"New trainer, first time blinkers."

"It's 25-1, Ray."

"Not any more. It's down to 16's. Someone likes it. And it's well drawn for a front runner."

"Look, it's fine. Do you have a calculator? I just can't work out what I've won. The numbers won't fix in my …"

"A couple more minutes. Let's just watch this, together, then I'll work it out. You've had a good day, Nick, whatever happens. A really good day."

It was about to get even better.

The race took one minute and eight seconds to unfold. Apple Tree Yard broke with alacrity from the inside stall and quickly established a three length lead. The favourite tried to pull alongside as they approached the final bend, but was sending out distress signals even before they hit the straight. Nothing was gaining from the pack and Apple Tree Yard seemed to gain momentum as the curve unwound, hugging the inside rail and powering clear unchallenged.

"Well I never," Ray said, placing a hand on my shoulder and squeezing gently.

I became still and quiet as the race unfolded. I didn't quite believe what I was seeing. I suppose I was elated, but the feeling struggled to get out. It was as though it didn't really know where to go.

Ray produced an old bottle of Bell's from a cupboard somewhere and poured some into a plastic cup. Passing it to me, he said, "Take this out the back. Have a drink, get some air. I'll join you in a minute."

I nodded dumbly and did as I was told. I went out of the fire exit into a small concrete yard lined with bins and discarded catering boxes. There was some cloud above, but not much. The air was cool and sweet. The whisky tasted harsh and burned my throat but I drank it all anyway. My thoughts and feelings refused to coalesce.

Ray joined me just as I finished my drink. He closed the door carefully behind him and passed me a piece of paper. I read the figure he'd written and smoothed the paper out and read it again. "Seriously?"

"Seriously," he said. "We pay a ten per cent bonus if you get all five up. I'd forgotten about it, to be honest. I mean, it hardly ever happens."

I looked at the figure again. A giddying rush of adrenaline swept through me.

"I'll need to call head office," Ray was saying. "They'll probably want to meet up, sort out some promotional shots ..."

"No," I said quickly. "I don't want anything like that. Can't it be anonymous, like with the lottery?"

"Sure, Nick. No problem. I'll sort it out." He laid a hand on my arm. "You're shaking. Look, I'm closing up in a minute, do you want to go for a drink?"

"Thanks, but I need to ..." I didn't know what I needed to do. "Thanks, Ray," I said again. "I'll see you all right, you know, I'll give ..."

"Don't worry about that. Just ..." He surveyed the unlovely contents of the yard and took a long breath. "This is your chance, Nick. To make a fresh start. You've been banging on about getting your own place, haven't you? Well, now you can."

"Jesus. I can, can't I?"

But I didn't.

*

155

Ray told me how and when I'd be receiving my winnings and assured me again that nobody else needed to know. We shook hands before I left. His grip was firm. Before he released it he said, "Nothing personal, Nick, but I hope I don't see you again."

I knew what he meant and I knew also that it was kindly intended, but I felt oddly hurt. "No point coming back, I suppose. I can't match this, can I? Ever."

"No," he said simply and turned and went back into the shop.

I walked the long way home. I waited for my thoughts to settle, but they were having none of it. I briefly considered forgetting about the anonymity, and boasting about my achievement; to Mum, to Hannah, Jessica and to Patrick. Especially to Patrick. I wanted to rub his face in it, tell him I could lend him a few quid if he was short, what with him out of work and a baby on the way. I let that thought play out in my mind for a few delicious moments. Then I stopped dead outside the Co-Op on Earlham Road and said out loud, "What achievement?"

An elderly man, walking a small, scruffy mongrel, gave me an understandably wary look as he passed, giving me as much space on the pavement as he could. I laughed and heard his footsteps quicken as he walked away from me.

It was sheer, dumb luck; a once in several lifetimes lightning strike of good fortune. That was all. I'd keep it to myself; this was my instinct anyway, in respect of most things; truth, lies, feelings. It was nobody else's business.

When I finally got home the first thing my mum said was, "You've missed your tea. And you stink of booze."

"And how was *your* day?" I said, but I was speaking to her back as she bustled out of the kitchen. I can leave this place, I thought. I got myself a glass of milk and sat at the table. I heard the television playing in the living room; *Antiques Roadshow*, one of my mother's perennial Sunday evening favourites.

I sat and sipped cold milk and mulled over the prospects and possibilities afforded by my windfall. It was odd then, that as I mulled, as I considered, my thoughts became longer and darker and coiled in on themselves, and that I was left, as I stared into my empty glass, with a single conviction; the money I'd won, a fraction under five figures, was lovely, fantastic, really, and I was grateful, of course I was, but ... it wasn't enough.

Chapter 24

There's a Sainsbury's on the outskirts of King's Lynn and I drive towards it. My head does not clear. It is full of discordant images, alongside miniscule shards of atomised memories. I don't trust any of it. Patrick's voice is there too, along with my mother's, and I don't trust them either. I think I can smell my father's scent; it is stale and acrylic, a hint of a long-discontinued cologne. I'm aware that this is probably a false memory, if indeed it is my memory at all. Perhaps I have misappropriated it from my brother, if one can assimilate a memory from somebody else. I don't know. I am not at all sure that I care.

The shopping doesn't take long and neither does the drive back to Ivy's cottage. She is effusively grateful when I hand her the single bag. I offer to put it away for her but she brushes that off and totters through to the kitchen with the bag in hand.

I sit next to Jessica on the sofa and hand her the keys. "Thanks. Everything okay?"

"Just peachy." She pushes a strand of hair away from her face in a way that reminds me of Hannah. "She shouldn't be on her own."

"What, Ivy?"

"Of course, Ivy. Who else would I be talking about?"

"I don't know. I ..."

"I'm sorry," she says quickly, her hand on my

arm. I feel its pressure through my coat, my sweater, my shirt. "I didn't mean to snap."

"That's okay. I just wish there was an adult here, that's all."

"We're adults, Nick."

"Yeah. Well. About that."

She releases my arm with a brisk pat. "Don't worry. I'll make some calls."

"You will?"

"I'm not sure who to … but how hard can it be?" I sense her hesitate. "And Nick, there's …"

Ivy comes back in brandishing a pair of twenty pound notes. She tries to pass them to me. "It's fine, Ivy. It was nowhere near that much."

"Still. You went out of your way. You must take something."

"We've had tea and biscuits and a lovely chat. You've had a tough time of it the last couple of weeks. This is my treat."

She sits with difficulty and lays the notes on the table with the tea things. "Are you sure? It's very kind. Very like Patrick." She looks uncomfortable. "This nice lady …"

"Jessica," Jessica says.

"*Jessica*. She says that you're Patrick's brother?"

"That's right."

Her hands twist together in her lap. "Are you sure? Patrick said that he didn't have a brother. He said he *had* one, but …"

"But, what?"

"He died. Very young, Patrick said. Just an infant, really. Car crash. Him and his father. Patrick's father. They were hit by a drunk driver, he said. Just another tragedy, he said. He thought perhaps they were cursed. The whole family. I told him that was nonsense. No such things as curses. Things go up and things go down, but they always come around in the end. That's what I told him and he smiled and said that he was sure I was right." She leans forward and extends a hand towards mine. "It's Nicholas, isn't it, dear?"

"Yes."

"Was Patrick lying to me? Why would he do that, do you think?"

"No. He wasn't lying. I'm his *step*-brother, Ivy. It's just a misunderstanding, that's all."

"*Step*-brother. I see. That explains it, doesn't it? I didn't think he would lie. Not Patrick. Not to me."

Jessica turns towards me and I feel her breath upon my face. "Yes, Ivy. That explains it."

A little later, standing by the car, after we've said our goodbyes and assured Ivy that we'll let her know when we've located Patrick, Jessica says, "That was kind."

"What?"

"The step-brother thing. Sparing her feelings like that."

"Kind? Sure. Of course, it might be true. I mean who the fuck knows?"

"Nick."

"Seriously. Who knows? Could be that my grandparents were war criminals, so all bets are off, really, aren't they?"

"Nick. Come on. She's an old woman and Patrick is …"

"Yes?"

"Well, Patrick is Patrick."

"What else did she have to say? Ivy. When I was doing the shopping?"

"Apparently she doesn't get around as well as she used to."

"It's not funny. What did she say?"

"I don't know. It looks like he's been kicked out of the house. Bailiffs have been round; changed the locks, picked the place clean."

"About the family. What did she have to say about my family, Hannah?"

"Hannah?"

"What?"

"You called me Hannah?"

"I didn't."

"You really did."

"I wouldn't do that, Jessica."

"Just get in the car."

"I'm sorry ..."

"It's not just that. The way you spoke to me just now? Not acceptable, Nick."

I get in the car and so does she. The drive home takes around an hour. It feels much longer.

Chapter 25

Three weeks after my big win I was back in the Ladbrokes on Unthank Road and Ray was fixing me with a look that was almost hostile. He couldn't maintain it, though; his eyes were too soft, his nature too kind.

"Just a social call, I assume?" he said, producing a tea from somewhere and passing it to me. It was as predictably awful as always, which was a comfort.

"Something like that." It was a Thursday morning, a nothing day in the racing world and the shop was all but empty. It felt good to be back, though, amongst the lost and the mediocre. "How are things? You're looking good."

"Yeah, I've got a mirror at home. I know exactly how I look. Have you got your own place yet?"

I shuffled on the spot and drank some tea. "About that. I haven't really got enough, mate." Ray looked at me; his moustache was still, his face impassive. "Not to buy outright. Not in today's market."

"Heck of a deposit, though."

"Yeah, but ... that's my capital gone, isn't it?"

"Capital?"

"Yeah, the strangest thing, I met an old friend this weekend. At a funeral, of all things ..."

I told him about Dan, the builder, about how I was going into business with him.

"What do you know about the building trade?"

"Nothing. Don't need to. Dan knows all that stuff. I'm just the ..."

"The what, Nick?"

"The money guy," I said weakly. "Anyway, I can learn."

"I'm sure you can."

He was starting to piss me off. "Come on, Ray. You're harshing my buzz."

"I beg your pardon?"

"It's an expression. It's something young people say."

"I see. Anyway, it was nice catching up, but I've got to get on."

"Cool. Just sling us another tea and the *Racing Post*, will you?"

"The *Racing Post*?"

"Yep. It's a paper, mostly involved with horse racing. I really thought you'd know that."

"Funny man," he said, throwing a copy in my direction.

I opened it, smoothed out a page. "Look, it's different this time. I've got a plan. And a bank. A betting bank. One bet a day, five per cent of the bank, win or lose. It can't go wrong."

"It can, Nick. You know it can."

"Yeah, but not for ages." He didn't return my smile.

I took the hint and studied the form for a while on my own. Then I went for a walk and had some lunch and got back to Ladbrokes in time to place my one bet of the day. I watched it lose by a short head. I had another bet and then another. It was busier now and I waited until Ray was otherwise engaged and placed my bets with his colleague, Jane, an anxious, middle-aged woman, who, mercifully, avoided eye contact or any prolonged conversation. By three o'clock I'd lost just over half of my supposed bank. I waited until Ray wasn't looking and snuck out into the bright, gormless day. My cheeks burned in the cool air.

Chapter 26

Jessica drops me off at my door. I suggest a drink or an early dinner, but she's having none of it. It's a relief, getting out of the car and away from the atmosphere that has grown between us. The relief fades quickly as she drives away and I miss her the moment she is out of sight.

The flat is empty. My mind isn't. It is crammed and busy and buzzing and I don't know what to do. Coherent thoughts refuse to form. I switch the TV on and tune the channel to live racing from Newbury. I watch the horses negotiate a single hurdle then turn the TV off again. The Ladbrokes on Unthank Road, is open, I think. I could go and see Ray. I imagine the look on his face. I put my coat on and leave the flat again. The light is dying and the wind is brisk and bitter. I head for Unthank Road and then change direction.

My mother is in the kitchen, preparing crab paste rolls. She stands with her back to me, at the sink, washing a cucumber. The table is set for one. A half-empty glass of sweet sherry rests next to a plate containing a cross-section of dry-looking fruit cake. "So you have seen Patrick, then."

"I didn't say that."

"You called me 'Fraulein'. Which I assume is your idea of a joke."

"It's no joke."

"No. It isn't."

"It's not that I care. About being German. I'm not prejudiced. Not like you."

"You're not German. Don't flatter yourself." She brings the cucumber across to the table, drying it on a piece of kitchen paper and cutting it into thick chunks. The smell of it, fresh, green, vegetal, fills the room. "I'm disappointed. In Patrick. All these years ... why now? What's the point?" She wipes her hands unnecessarily on a tea towel and then throws it across the table. She looks at me for the first time since I'd entered the room. "I'm not ashamed."

"I didn't say ..."

"There's no shame, boy, don't you ever go thinking that. We didn't tell you because you couldn't take it. Patrick could. Patrick understood, but you ... even as a baby, so *sensitive*, so *needy*. We agreed, Patrick and I. Our secret. The family name had long gone. Mother and father ... they had no choice. They came here on forged papers. A new life. But they found out. The *Jews*. They *always* find out." She shrugs. "And so. New names. *Another* life."

"What did they do?"

"Do?"

"To need forged papers. To have to change their identity. It wasn't a crime to be German. Was it? What did they do?"

She pulls her shoulders straight. There is fire in her face and in her eyes. "Nothing. They did nothing. Were they in the party? Yes. In the fatherland, in those days, if you wanted any kind of life, you joined the party. The country was better, in many ways, they said. Until ..."

"Until, what?"

"Who are you to judge? With your central heating

and your easy life. You have no idea what their lives were like. Bread made with sawdust. Coffee brewed from acorns. And the cold ..."

"What did they do?"

"He was a guard. Papa. At one of the camps. One of the little camps." She purses her lips and makes a gesture. As though this is nothing and she doesn't understand what all the fuss is about. "They just made them work, that's all, that's what papa said."

"My grandfather was a guard at a concentration camp?"

"It was a *work* camp. You never listen, Nicholas, that's why ..." She cuts herself off with an angry huff and walks over to the kitchen window, snatching the curtains together with a single jerk. "When they came, when the *American's* came, they made the people from the village ... tidy up."

"Tidy up?"

"Mama among them. They had her digging up ... among all the stench and disease ... digging and dragging ... her ... mamma ..." She pulls a tissue from the pocket of her housecoat and dabs at her eyes.

"Digging up what? Bodies? You said it was a work camp?"

"It was bombed. The allies. There was disease ... some things cannot be helped. You believe all the stories, of course, all the propaganda." She puts the tissue away again. Her eyes are entirely dry. "She was related to the mayor, you know. She was somebody. She wore fine clothes. They looked up to her, in the village. They had money. Some influence. So they were able to get out. They could be shot, Papa said, any moment. To come here, of course, to end up here ... but they had to keep running until ... here. The enemy. Still, to live is to live."

"Jesus. I can't take this."

She turns on me. "Of course you can't. That's why we didn't tell you."

"It's not your fault. Who your parents are, what they did. You could have explained. Talked to us both. Together. We could have been ..." My voice falters.

"Been, what? A happy family? With you and your degenerate gambling and your women? Anyway, I do not apologise for my family and that's what you want, isn't it? You want me to grovel. Well, I won't. I'm proud of Papa and of Mama. I wouldn't expect you to understand that."

"Probably just as well."

"So where is he? Your brother? I will be having words with him. I expected better. Such a disappointment, but I suppose he is a man, after all."

"I don't know where he is."

"What are you talking about?"

"He's been kicked out of his house. Couldn't pay the rent. He could be anywhere."

"So where did you get all this ... information from?"

"His neighbour. She's your generation, actually. A bit older, perhaps. But, decent. Kind. And Patrick was kind to her, believe it or not."

"He gossiped to a stranger? About me? About us?" Her face is the colour of skimmed milk.

"I wasn't sure I even believed it, considering the other bollocks he told her. Thanks for the confirmation, though."

"Get out." I have seen her fury before, but this time I relish it.

"What about Patrick? Aren't you worried? He's ill, apparently. And presumably he's living on the streets so ..."

"Patrick is not my son. Neither are you. Get out."
Her voice becomes quieter as her anger grows. By the
time she says it again I can barely hear her at all. "Get
out."

I am happy to do as I am told.

Chapter 27

A couple of days after my visit to the bookies and fresh from a meeting with Dan, I got a call on my mobile. I didn't recognise the number, but I answered it anyway. It was a welcome distraction from the thought of physical work and of actually having to earn a living.

I didn't recognise the voice at first. It was shrill, hysterical. "Nick? Where have you been? You left me. With him."

"Hannah?"

"I'm using a *burner*, Nick. A *burner*. Like a bloody drug dealer."

"A burner?"

"A pay as you go. I can't use my phone, he'll check. He checks everything."

"Jesus, Hannah. I'm sorry."

"Where were you?"

"I couldn't … I thought you needed some space. You just said … if I'd called, he'd have known."

"You could have warned me, Nick. You *should* have warned me. Years ago." She no longer sounded hysterical. Her voice was a tiny, broken thing.

"What's he done?"

"Will you meet me? He's away next week. Golf. Some old contacts who he thinks will give him a job."

"Tell me where and when." She did. "Are you at work?"

"I've been signed off for a bit. Look, I've got to go. If he finds this phone, I'm *fucked*."

"I'll speak to him ..."

"NO!" Her voice was so loud I instinctively pulled my phone away from my ear. "Don't say anything to anybody. Please. Just meet me next week."

She rang off.

We met at Holkham, in a car park next to a wood that led to the beach. I was on time but Hannah's Clio was already there. She leant against the driver's door, pale, but elegant, in a light jacket and sunglasses and a honey-coloured silk scarf. She wore boots and a long skirt. She seemed over-dressed, I thought. It was late spring and the day was mild and still. I was shocked to see that she was smoking.

"Hannah?" I said, approaching her.

She looked at the cigarette and seemed surprised to see it there. "I don't even smoke." She tossed the cigarette to the ground and stamped it to pieces. "I don't even like it. Stupid, stupid ..."

"It's okay," I said, reaching for her.

She flinched away from my touch. "Don't tell anyone. Not even Jessica. *Especially* Jessica. Another secret." Her voice was atonal, her smile all over the place.

"Not a word. I promise."

"You are a prince," she said. I tried to move closer but she shuffled away, maintaining the distance between us. "I would quite like a hug. But at the same time ... I really don't want anyone to touch me."

"Okay."

"It's a difficult circle to square. I appreciate that."

"What happened, Hannah?"

"What happened?" She appeared distracted. It

was a small car park and ours were the only cars in it. She removed her jacket and laid it over the top of her Clio.

"Hannah?"

She put a finger to pursed lips, then grabbed the hem of her powder-blue sweater and pulled it upwards until it reached her chin. Her bra was white and lacy and, to my shame, it was this and the hint of nipple beneath the lace that I noticed before I saw the bruises.

"Christ," I said. She stood quite still and didn't speak. The bruises, mottled, plum-coloured, turning yellow-green in places, spread from just above the waistband of her skirt on the right hand side to her ribcage. They were obscured by the line of her bra. As far as I could see they curled around to her back, possibly her buttocks.

"They're starting to fade," she said, matter of factly. "They're a week old." She took off her sunglasses and her eyes settled on mine. "These are a bit older." She placed a tentative finger on a swelling underneath her left eye. "A bit of make-up and you'd barely notice."

"I'm sorry," I said, remembering the feel of Patrick's hand against the side of my head. I thought of Hannah cringing, cowering away from him. I felt anger, of course, and a deep sense of shame.

She pulled her sweater down again and smoothed it against her stomach. She put her jacket on and her sunglasses. "You could have warned me, Nick."

"I did. Once."

"But that was too late. Far too late. I was years in. There was no going back. Not then."

"And now?"

"Now?"

"You've got to leave. And call the police."

"Leave?" she said, as though she hadn't heard the

word before. "Can we walk to the beach? I fancy an ice cream."

"Sure thing," I said. She'd caught me off guard and was already striding towards the trees. I had to trot to catch her up.

We walked through the pine wood, to the beach. To our left lay acres of fields, packed with raucous, restless geese. Every now and then a flock of them would explode skyward, wheeling and scattering against a buttermilk sky.

The day was still and quiet and as the woods grew thicker the more hushed the air became. "It's like a cathedral," Hannah said; the first words she'd spoken since we'd left the car park.

She side-stepped a fallen tree and I followed her. "Kind of."

She was walking with purpose and I was struggling to keep up. She stopped suddenly and waited for me. She surprised me by reaching out an arm so that I could take her hand. "The thing is, I was careless. He told me to stop taking the pill and I said I would. Of course, I didn't, but he found out. That was the first time he hit me." I started to say something but she gripped my hand tighter. "It's fine, Nick. Just don't let go."

A glade opened up briefly and there was a hint of pale sun. Then the trees thickened again and the path narrowed. It was a longer walk to the beach than I had imagined.

"We used to come here when we were kids," Hannah said. "The four of us. Before ... well, before. It's nice, isn't it?"

"It's lovely."

"I don't know why he hit me the second time. He'd been drinking, I suppose. He was angry. But then he's always drinking, always angry … so, go figure, as the American's say."

"I'm not sure Patrick needs a reason for anything."

"He was nice afterwards, though. Almost kind."

"A slap one day, an ice cream the next," I said.

"What?"

"Nothing."

"He felt guilty, I suppose. Or as guilty as Patrick gets. The thing is, he is very determined to … procreate."

"What do you mean?"

"And it's fair to say I'm not exactly in the mood. Not under the current circumstances."

I stopped walking and she stopped too. She kept hold of my hand. "That's rape, isn't it?" I said, appalled.

"I'm not sure I'd call it that."

"What would you call it?"

"I'm not sure I'd call it anything."

We walked again and moments later we reached the beach.

Chapter 28

I stand outside the Ladbrokes on Unthank Road, in a cold, lifeless, drizzle, waiting for it to open.

"You're late," I say when Ray finally gets around to it. I hear the key turn and see the sign flip from "closed" to "open" and I push my way in. He's halfway back to the counter. He turns on his heel and faces me and says, very quietly, "Fuck off, Nick."

"Is that any way to ..."

"Seriously. Fuck off." I'm not sure it's the real Ray. The white shirt is unpressed, the tie as wayward as ever ... but his eyes are cold and even his moustache seems distant and forbidding.

I wipe rainwater from my forehead and hair. "Come on, Ray ..."

"How long has it been?"

"How long has it been since, what?"

"You had a bet, Nick. What do you think?"

"I don't know. Who says I haven't been betting? This isn't the only shop in town and there's this little thing called the Internet ..."

"It's three months." He's behind the counter again now. He checks his watch. "A little more than that, actually. You can break a habit in three months. You can beat an addiction."

"That's great, but ..."

"You're not having a bet in here, Nick."

"You can't do that."

"I can."

"There's a William Hill just around the corner. I'll go in there."

"You do what you like. It's a free country. But you're not having a bet in here."

"Jesus, Ray. Maybe I only came in to see how you are."

"Really, Nick? Is that what this is? A social call?" My hesitation says everything and he turns back to his computer screen, shaking his head. He looks up a moment later and sees that I haven't left. "What?"

"I don't know what else to do. I don't know where to go."

Finally his expression softens. "You know the café round the corner? Jane's coming in soon, so I can have a break at about twelve. I'll meet you there. We can have a proper cup of tea."

"Okay."

"In a big mug. Something you can stand your spoon up in. It'll put hairs on your chest."

"Great."

"But until then ..."

"What?"

"What I said earlier."

"You told me to fuck off."

"I did."

"You don't even swear, Ray."

"Not very often, no."

He makes a shooing gesture with his arms and I walk back out into the rain.

The imaginatively named *Unthank Café* sits between a florist and a newsagent. It has a glass-rich frontage that juts aggressively into the street. I take a seat at the front and clear a smeary circle in the thick rime of condensation that has formed on the inside of the long, high window. The view afforded me is blurred and unspectacular; a wet, mainly unpeopled pavement, a pedestrian crossing. An array of large, Victorian terraced houses loom opposite, mostly converted into student accommodation. I am served a mug of undeniably strong builder's tea. I think of Tash, of the afternoons we spent in her shabby, chilly, student digs. I think of her bedroom, the smell of it, the faded and stained patina of her old quilt. I think of her body, of course, but only briefly, because thoughts like these can lead nowhere good. The little viewing portal I've created is already misting over. I leave it be and drink my tea and wait for Ray.

The place is almost full by the time he gets here. It's filled with a comfortable bubble of myriad conversations that blend and compress into a warm hum. The air is soaked with predictable scents; bacon, coffee, the tart acidity of tomatoes frying.

"I told you it was strong," Ray says, as he squeezes into the seat next to me. He's fetched his own mug of tea. He chinks it against mine. The liquid is thick and viscous, the colour of old teak.

"You could treat fence posts with this. God knows what it's doing to my insides."

"It's good for the soul," Ray says. He cradles his hands around his chipped, red mug. He's wearing a quilted coat over his Ladbrokes gear, zipped to the throat. "I'm sorry about earlier."

"Are you?"

The briefest pause. "No. Not in the slightest."

"The thing is …"

"It doesn't matter. Don't have a bet."

"I'm sorry? You have no idea what I was going to say."

"Some problem or other, I dare say. Some kind of

drama. No offence, Nick, but that's usually the size of it." I start to speak but he cuts me off. "The details are irrelevant. The answer is, don't have a bet."

"As simple as that?"

"Simple as that. Three months. That's something. Keep on doing what you're doing and things will get better."

"Better? Do you know how shit my life is right now? Don't you even want to know ..."

"No one cares. Seven billion stories, mate, what makes yours so special?"

"Jesus, Ray."

"So things are shit. Why shouldn't they be? All I'm saying is, you start gambling again and they'll get worse."

"I might win."

"You won't."

"I did once."

"Did you? Ultimately?"

I take a heavy breath and stare into my empty mug. "What are you? Some kind of Zen fucking bookie, with your advice and your tea and ..." The tenuous thread that was holding the thought together breaks.

"Something like that. Look, I know some of what's going on; you and Hannah breaking up. I know that Patrick's missing."

"Jesus. How?"

"It's a small city. And people gossip, especially in a bookies."

"I thought nobody cared?"

"They don't. That doesn't mean they don't like to talk." He leans back in his seat and raises an arm towards the counter. "I'm ordering some grub. Do you want anything?" I shake my head. "Don't know what you're missing." A thin, cheerful-looking woman in a wrap-around apron makes her way over. Ray flirts clumsily with her and orders his usual. "Janice," he says as he turns back towards me. "Wonderful woman. Putty in my hands, of course."

"Of course."

"You've lost weight. I'll order you a full English, if you like? My treat?" I shake my head. "Shame. You could do with feeding up."

"You sound just like Jessica."

"Jessica?" He raises a forefinger. "Jessica? Hannah's sister?"

"That's right."

"You and her? Are you …"

"No. Nothing like that. Just friends."

"You were an item once, though, yes? Or do I misremember?"

"We were. But that was years ago."

"But, a rekindling? You'd welcome it? I can tell."

I shrug. "Too much water, too many bridges."

"Shame." Janice returns bearing a mound of bubble and squeak with two perfectly fried eggs balanced upon its peak. "Thank you, sweetheart," Ray says. He gives her forearm a gentle squeeze. She doesn't seem to mind.

"What would Mrs Ray think?" I say, once Janice has returned to the counter.

"I'll tell you a little secret." He shakes a bottle of HP sauce vigorously and then empties half of it over his lunch. "There is no Mrs Ray." He takes an enormous mouthful of food. His moustache bristles and jiggles as eats.

"Okay."

"There was. And a couple of little Rays. Once upon a time." He shovels more food in. He eats quickly but silently.

"I'm sorry."

He wipes flecks of egg and potato from his facial hair. "They've gone to a better place."

"Christ. I didn't …"

"Well, Stourbridge. I mean it's all relative, really, isn't it?" He starts eating again and I wait until he draws breath.

"What happened?"

There's a pause as he continues eating. "She met someone else. A better man. Someone who doesn't gamble."

"You gambled?"

Another hiatus, but he's slowing down now as his plate empties. "With both hands. Made you look like an amateur. Housekeeping, rent, pocket money for the boys, it was all the same to me. Funny thing is, it was her dad that put me onto it. He could handle it. I couldn't."

"It gets inside your blood."

"It does. It comes out again though. If you let it."

"But you work in a bookies?"

"I know. I suppose that's irony, huh?"

"How did that even happen?"

"Funny story." He unzips his jacket. It's warm in the café now, in the fug of food and conversation. "I did some cleaning for a while, after Irene left. To try and make ends meet. They didn't meet. They never do when you're gambling. But look who I'm telling. Anyway, I ended up cleaning that big old Ladbrokes on Ber Street, late in the evening, after all the punters had gone. I had to sweep up all the losing slips and empty the bins that were full to the brim with them. And I'd clean behind the counter as well, where they keep this folder with copies of all the winning bets. I looked at the size of that folder, how slim it was, and then I looked at this mountain of … loss. The scale of it …" He shakes his head. "I thought, even I'm not that much of a mug. So I stopped. Overnight."

"Just like that?"

"I haven't had a bet since."

"That doesn't explain how you ended up behind the counter."

"I got on well with the manager. He was a good guy, for a bookie. When I told him I was quitting as a cleaner he said his assistant had just handed his notice in and the job was mine, if I wanted it. It didn't seem a great idea, on the face of it, with my ... issues, and I told him so. He shrugged it off, said something about aversion therapy, poacher turned gamekeeper, all rubbish, of course, but ... he was persuasive. And I needed the work. The rest is history, as they say."

"Perhaps it wasn't rubbish? What he said. Aversion therapy?"

"Maybe not. I like the work. I don't like the punters. Most of them, anyway. They remind me too much of the old me, of what I had and what I threw away. I don't need them to put me off gambling, though. That part of me is dead. Dead and gone. Thank goodness."

"Are you still in touch? With your family, your kids?"

"No. I did try, once I'd ... got better. But Irene wasn't interested. I don't blame her. She was settled, she said. The kids were settled. She wasn't unkind, but she was firm. They're grown up now, the boys. Got jobs of their own, I suppose."

"Old enough to make their own decisions about who they see or who they don't see."

"Perhaps, but ... it's up to them. If they come looking for me one day, that's great. I don't think they will."

"I'm sorry."

"Don't be. It's the price I pay. Not just for the gambling, but also the lies and deceit that goes along with it. Consequences. That's all it is. We can do whatever the hell we like as long we're prepared to accept the consequences."

After a moment I ask him if he'd like another tea. He stands and zips up his coat and says, thanks but he has to get back to work. He's half-turned towards the door when he stops and says, "A funny thing; Jane. You know Jane?"

"Of course I know Jane."

"She's leaving. Handed her notice in."

"Okay. Well, I'm sure she'll be missed."

"I like to think she couldn't handle being around my sexual charisma all day, but actually she's got herself a job in Boots."

"Better hours, I assume? Better pay?"

"Almost certainly."

"Well, that's fascinating and I wish her well, of course, but ..."

"Are you looking for work?"

"Me?"

"Yes, Nick. You."

"You can't be serious. I'm not even sure I could do it."

"If Jane can do it, bless her, then so can you."

"You'd be my boss?"

"Technically. We wouldn't be working together all the time, but sometimes we would. What do you think?"

"I don't know what to say."

"It's funny, isn't it, how the circles turn?"

"Can I think about it?"

"Of course you can."

"Thank you, Ray. For the thought. You're a good guy," I say. "For a bookie."

I hold out my hand and he shakes it.

Chapter 29

"Isn't it lovely?" she said. The tide was out and the sand was soft and damp and tiny shells crunched beneath our feet. The sea was flat and colourless, the sky empty, preparing for dusk.

"You've got to leave, Hannah."

"And go where?"

"Jessica? Your parents?"

"They can't know. Not yet. Anyway, it's my house. It's *our* house. I'm not going anywhere." I started to say something but she cut me off. "And I'm not going to the police."

"What, then?"

She removed her sunglasses and stared out at the sea. There was no wind to speak of so it just sat there, flat and indifferent. "Ice creams are this way, I think," she said, shifting her gaze towards some dunes and a small scrub of trees.

We walked past the trees, still hand in hand, and came across some decking with a shop, a café and an open kiosk, ringed with sets of metallic tables and chairs, some of which spilled onto the beach. Hannah released my hand and took a seat. "I'll have a ninety-nine, please."

An elderly couple were being served at the kiosk. I took my place behind them. A young mother sat at one of the tables near Hannah. Her son – five or so, tousle-haired, impish – ran from table to table, drumming a brief tattoo with his fists on the surface of each. He stopped at Hannah's table and stared openly at the bruises on her face. Hannah turned her head away and slid her sunglasses back on. The boy eased back towards his mother. She pulled him onto her lap and whispered something into his ear. He squirmed and giggled.

"Do you want to walk again?" I said, handing Hannah her ice cream.

"Not yet. Let's sit." I did as I was told. "Are you not having one?" She extracted the small chocolate flake from the centre of her ice cream and studied it. "Just like mum. She'd never have one either. She didn't really like eating. Didn't approve. She worried about her weight, you see. Jessica would want a choc ice or a Mivvy; basically anything they didn't have. Typical Jessica; had to be awkward, had to be different. Drove dad mad. Drove us all mad, really."

"Hannah …"

"He's away until late Friday." She licked her ice cream and her brow furrowed. "I don't trust that, though. I expect he'll come back early, try and catch me out. Still, I've got a couple of days."

"A couple of days to do what?"

"Get the locks changed, sort out some security. Get his stuff together so I can dump it on the front lawn."

"He'll go ballistic."

"The third time he hit me, I … provoked him. It wasn't hard. I recorded it on my phone, what he did. Covertly, of course. It was difficult, trying to keep in the right position while he hit me, praying he wouldn't see the phone. I've taken pictures of my bruises as well, and audio recordings of some of his rants."

"But he goes through your phone …"

"And my laptop. He's hacked my email, of course.

But I've opened an account with one of those obscure providers. I did it through work. I've sent myself emails with the files attached and saved the drafts. There's no way he can find them. At least, I don't *think* he can." She dropped her ice cream onto the sand and wiped her fingers carefully. "So … he'll leave and he'll sign the house over to me and he won't see or speak to me again or I'll send it all to the police. The whole lot, just like that."

"Do you think … I'm not sure he'll buy it, Hannah."

"He will. He has too. If he doesn't I'll tell everyone. *Show* everyone. He won't be able to bear it; the humiliation."

We sat for a while. Hannah was calm and quiet, her hands folded neatly in her lap.

"I still think …"

"You'll come back with me, won't you? Tonight?"

"Come back with you?"

"To the house. You hate living with your mum, don't you? You've wanted to move out for ages."

"You want me to move in with you?" God knows how gormless I looked. The incredulity was almost too much. I was struggling to take it in.

"Of course." She looked at me over the top of her sunglasses. "I can't do this on my own, Nick."

Chapter 30

It's Saturday, early afternoon, and I'm eating dry toast and drinking instant coffee when there's a knock at the door. I'm surprised, when I open it, to see Jessica standing on the top step, arms folded demurely in front of her. The day outside is quiet and calm. There's some cloud, but it's low and thin and a brief smear of sunlight slides across Jessica's cheek and onto my face.

"You've done something to your hair," I say. It's shorter, straighter.

She touches the side of her head self-consciously. "Bless you for noticing."

I see that her car is parked at an angle opposite and that the engine is running. "You not staying?"

She glances back at the car as though she's forgotten that it's there. "Not at this precise moment. But ... I did wonder ... does your offer still stand?"

"Offer?"

"Christ, Nick. Can I still move in? For a while, at least. Give me a chance to look for something else."

"Yes. Of course. But to honest, I didn't think ..."

"I know. But, look, Steve's moving in. With Hannah. Things have ... escalated. I couldn't stay there if I wanted to. And anyway, she's giving me a hard time. She knows I've been hanging out with you. She's using words like Judas and traitor."

"Oh."

She shrugs. "Just Hannah being Hannah. The thing is, the other day, you were a prick."

"I know. I'm sorry …"

"But you'd had a shock. And I shouldn't have sulked. That's what Tabitha said and she's right."

"Good old Tabitha."

"How are things? Any sign of Patrick?" I shake my head and tell her about my conversation with my mother. "Fuck, Nick. I'm sorry."

"For what? I think … the truth is, I have no idea what to think."

"Look, I've got to go, but my plan is, I bring my stuff back later, we'll have a takeaway and a catch up. Then tomorrow we can go and see Ivy, check up on her. I made some calls. Social services can't get involved unless she knows about it. So let's have a chat with her and persuade her that she needs some help."

"Sounds good. And it's really nice of you, Jessica. About Ivy, I mean."

"Is it? She'll probably hate me for it. Still … we couldn't just leave her." She heads towards her car, but then checks herself and comes back up the steps and gives me a hug. "Thanks, mate," she says. "For putting me up."

I hold on tightly. I have to make myself let her go. "What are friends for?"

She presses dry lips quickly against my cheek. "I'll be back by teatime. It's going to be great." She looks over my shoulder into the interior of my flat. "Cosy, but great."

Chapter 31

We drove straight back to Hannah's from the beach at Holkham. We ate toast and drank tea and didn't speak much. It felt so unreal it was as though I was watching myself; I was an actor performing a role. What words I spoke were scripted, albeit not particularly well. I was a stiff, alien presence in a, mostly, unfamiliar house. Patrick was everywhere. Naturally. This was his house, after all. But not just physically – an array of coats in the hallway, boots and shoes, a handful of golfing magazines sprawled across the coffee table – every room carried his scent, his testosterone-stench, the sense of territories firmly marked.

Hannah had left her phone at home. Patrick had put a tracker on it, she said, so if she'd taken it with her he would know where she'd been. He'd forbidden her to leave the house whilst he was away. He'd left messages, of course, several of them, each increasingly irritable and then downright angry. She went into the garden to call him back; I watched her through the living room window, silhouetted in the half-light, pacing from path to tree to flowerbed, head bowed, phone clamped to her ear. When she came in she was pale and her hands were shaking.

"I told him the phone was on charge and I was in the garage, defrosting the freezer."

"Did he buy it?"

"I don't know. Possibly. As long as he stays away for two more days it doesn't matter." She threw the phone on the sofa and slumped down next to it. "He was more interested in whether I've had my period yet."

I almost asked the obvious question, but managed to stop myself. "I'm sorry."

"I haven't, by the way. But then it's not due yet. You'd think he'd know that, wouldn't you?" Unsure what to say, I grunted sympathetically. She patted the cushion next to her. "Will you be okay on here tonight?"

"Of course. Look, are you sure this is a good idea?"

"What?"

"It's just ..."

"I thought you cared about me, Nick."

"I do, Hannah. Of course, I do, but ..."

"He's miles away. There's no need to be scared."

"I'm not scared," I lied.

It was a long night. The sofa was not particularly comfortable. Every time I heard a noise outside I thought it might be Patrick, home early to catch Hannah out. I tried to imagine how things would play out if he burst in and found me lying on the sofa. I couldn't. The thoughts wouldn't form. I thought also of the bruises on Hannah's flank and back; and then of her flat, smooth stomach and the curve of her breasts. It seemed incredible that she was lying only yards away from me. I heard her in the night a couple of times, her footsteps above, the sound of the bathroom door opening then closing again. I imagined her at the top of the stairs, calling down, asking me to join her. I wondered what I would say if she did. I didn't know. It hadn't been scripted yet.

*

I eventually fell into a deep sleep. I was shaken from it by Hannah. I woke reluctantly. Hannah was showered and dressed already; strands of her damp hair grazed across my face as she leant over me. The scents of shower gel and shampoo mingled; coconut, lime and something else; apricot perhaps. "Come on, sweetheart, up you get. Shower and dressed and we'll plan our day."

Sweetheart? I pondered that as I did what I was told.

When I came down a little later Hannah was sat at the kitchen table, hunched over her phone. She looked up at me and smiled. There was a cafetiere of coffee in the middle of the table and she told me to help myself. The locks would be changed by this afternoon, she said, and a security firm was coming first thing tomorrow. It was costing extra, what with the urgency and all, but what the hell. A strand of hair kept falling across her eye and the right side of her face and she was continually brushing it way and tucking it behind an ear. She was fresh-faced, no make-up; her bruises were visible. The ghosts of them, at least.

"Are you going to pick your stuff up?" she said. "From your mum's?"

"We're really doing this? I'm moving in?"

"Sure. Why not?" I didn't know what to say to that. "It'll be fun." I didn't know what to say to that either, so I sat opposite her and poured myself some coffee. "Look, you're getting cold feet, I get it."

"I'm not getting cold feet."

"I just need you for a few days. Then I'll release you back into the wild." She was trying to sound as though she was joking, but she wouldn't look at me and she was doing that thing with her hair again.

"I'm here for you, Hannah. I'm just ... adjusting, that's all."

"Adjusting. I remember adjusting when your brother punched me in the face."

"Hannah. Jesus."

"Sorry, Nick." She stood suddenly. "I've got some calls to make. I'll let you adjust." Coffee spilled from her mug as she pushed away from the table. She stopped at the kitchen door and turned back towards me. She came back to the table and stood by my side. She laid a hand on my shoulder then almost instantly removed it again. "I'm sorry. I'm not being fair."

"I just ... I can't believe what he's done, that's all."

"You've seen the bruises, Nick. I've got the photos."

"I believe you, of course I do. That's not what I mean. I suppose ... I didn't think he was capable. Not of this."

"Seriously?"

"Seriously. I'm under no illusions, Hannah. I know what kind of man by brother is, I know at first hand. But, it was always ..." I linked my hands around the coffee mug, as though to draw warmth from it. "Look, when he was in his teens, there were incidents; at least three, possibly more. He should have a record, by all accounts, could have gone to prison, if anyone had ever pressed charges. But they didn't."

"So why don't you ..."

"It was always other men. That he hit. I know it's misguided bullshit, Hannah ... but I never thought my brother would ever hit a woman."

"That's sweet." Her voice was so dry it was barely there. "It's funny how people can keep on surprising you, isn't it?"

"Look, I'm going to mine. I'll pick up some stuff, talk to mum."

"You can't talk to your mum, Nick. She'll warn him."

"I've got to say something ..."

"You can't." She was almost shouting. A hand tugged at the sleeve of my shirt then released it again. "You can't. Not yet. Please."

"Okay. Maybe I'll get lucky and she won't even be there."

Chapter 32

I watch Jessica as she drives away. I leave the front door open for a while, to air the place out. A vivid slice of sunlight illuminates the entrance mat and an isosceles of faded grey carpet. The air tastes sweet and mild. I feel a sudden thrill of energy and a sense of something that I can only assume is optimism. On a whim, I call Richard. He seems surprised to hear from me and his voice sounds wary, as though he's braced for bad news. I tell him what I know about Patrick. It isn't much, but he appreciates the update. The call gets easier after that and we agree to meet for a drink in the next week or two. It's nothing definite, but it's something; a bridge under construction, a wall crumbling.

I embark on some rudimentary housework. I change the bed sheets with a flourish and gather blankets and spare pillows in readiness for my migration to the sofa. Later, I shower and shave and change my clothes. I feel a growing nervousness as the afternoon runs down.

Jessica returns at a little after five. "What larks," she says as I open the door. She has a bottle of Prosecco in one hand and a holdall in the other. I am very aware of her scent as she squeezes past me. "I've got a few bin bags of clothes and stuff in the car. Give us a hand?"

After we've unloaded the Micra we sit in my living room. We're surrounded by over-filled black bags. "I'll have a sort out in a minute," Jessica says, as she pours us some wine. "And I'm on the sofa." I start to say something, but she raises a hand. "No arguments. You're doing me the favour here. I'm not kicking you out of your own bed."

"And there's me trying to be a gentleman."

"It's a bit late for that, mate." She raises her tumbler full of Prosecco and touches it to mine. "Cheers. You've had a shave. And is that Aramis I smell?"

"A little. Just making an effort. Don't worry, I haven't forgotten; terms and conditions. You've changed your clothes, I notice. And is that make up? And perfume?"

"A little. Just making an effort," she mimics. Her smile is angled as she tilts her head to one side. Her eyes flick away from mine. "Anyway, I'm celebrating. Getting away from my fucking sister. Jesus. I honestly thought only one of us was getting out of that house alive."

"So now it's Hannah and Steve. What would Patrick think? Yet another man taking up residence in his precious house."

"Who knows? Who cares? I still wonder where he is, though."

"I called some of the homeless shelters, gave a description, left my details. No dice."

"You tried."

"But not too hard. He's sick, isn't he? Perhaps he's doing what animals do when they're ill and near the end. Maybe he's crawled off somewhere to die."

"Jesus, Nick. You're killing the mood. I'm celebrating, remember?"

"Sorry." I take a mouthful of wine. The bubbles fizz up my nose and I sneeze twice, violently. "Sorry." I say again.

"Keeping it classy." She fiddles with her phone. "So what'll it be? Our takeaway? My treat."

"I'm not sure what I fancy? Indian? Chinese?"

"The eternal question. Let's split the difference and have a pizza."

"Why not?"

She concentrates on the screen of her phone. She's sitting in my chair, but I don't mind. She's compact and pretty in a burgundy sweater and pale jeans. She has her knees pressed together. Her face is tight with concentration as she places our order. The tip of her tongue juts out from the corner of her mouth. She brushes a hair from her eyes. She seems very vivid and real. "All done," she says, her head coming up. She sees me looking at her. "What?"

"Nothing. No anchovies, I trust?"

"No anchovies. I'm not an animal. The usual; a pepperoni and a margherita."

"The usual? When was the last time we ordered pizza together?"

"Dunno? Does it matter?" She consults her phone again then tucks it into the back pocket of her jeans. "Forty minutes, give or take."

"Nice one. Thanks, Jessica."

"My pleasure. By the way, guess who's got a job?"

"Call me crazy, but I'm guessing it's you."

"Give that man a biscuit. It's only temping, but still. And, yes ... temping was your idea. So ... well done."

"You took my advice? You sure you're still on your meds?"

"I'd forgotten how funny you are," she says dryly. "Yes. I'm taking my pills, like a good girl. Anyway, I've got a couple of weeks at one of those solicitors next to the Cathedral. It'll be the dregs, I know, bottom of the barrel stuff, but it's a start at least."

"I think it's great, Jessica. I'm chuffed for you." She reaches over with her glass again and chinks it against mine. "Actually, I have job news of my own."

"Seriously? We're going to need more Prosecco." I tell her about Ray's offer. She places her glass on the coffee table. "Okay. I mean, that's great and everything and I really don't want to piss on your chips, but are you sure that's such a great idea?"

"I know what you mean. I've been knocking it backwards and forwards all week." I tell her Ray's story; how he ended up in his job.

She picks up the glass again and drains it. "Could all be bullshit, mate. Just saying."

"I know, I know. But ... I'm not sure it matters. I think he means well, as far as I'm concerned. I don't know why, but there we are."

"Maybe you're the son he never had."

I hadn't mentioned Ray's children to Jessica and don't see the point in doing so now. "Maybe. And I've never had a father-figure so it all fits, but ... so what? I trust him, I think. I'm going to go for it, the job. Fuck it. I haven't even wanted a bet since he offered it to me. I feel ... lighter. Despite all that shit about Mum's family and Patrick ... it's like I've been dragging this weight around all my life, you know? This sense of ... *inertia*. Crushing me. But it's shifting now, I think. A little, at least. How about that? The fucking wonder of it."

"Jesus, Nick."

"Sorry. Bit heavy, huh?"

"No. It's fine. I said no bullshit. Anyway, I get it. It's family, man. That's what weighs us down. That's what Tabitha says and hey, it's nothing we didn't know, anyway, right?"

"Tabitha. Is she helping?"

"Like I said, it's a process. We're just sifting

through the debris, seeing what we find. Maybe I'll start feeling lighter soon, as well. That'd be pretty sweet."

"I'm sure you will. I hope so."

A little later the pizza comes and we eat it messily, straight from the box. We're debating whether to get more wine and laughing over something that Hannah once said, when Jessica looks suddenly pensive and says, "You know, I really hated it when you called me Hannah."

"So I gathered."

"I don't know why. I mean, I fucking hate the bitch, but … it was just a slip of the tongue."

"It was weird; it's not as if I even really think about her. And that in itself is odd, she was a big part of my life after all. We were together for …"

I hesitate and Jessica jumps in. "What?" she yelps. "You've forgotten? You can't even remember how long you and Hannah were together?"

"Of course I can. Don't be silly."

She looks delighted. "Jesus. Hannah would be so flattered. Come on, you must have had some good times?"

"Of course we did. One would assume. We went on holiday once. Tunisia."

"How was that?"

"It was shit. Far too hot. Hannah liked it, though. As far as I can remember."

She leans forward and presses a cool finger into the centre of my forehead. "You're so fucked, aren't you, mate?"

"Yeah. Probably. The thing is, one time, I was pretty sure I loved her. That makes no sense now; it's like it was another man, another me. It's all transactional, I suppose, relationships … especially with someone like Hannah, but …"

"But what?"

"Tash once said I've got a hole in the middle of me. I think she's right. Maybe, without that, Hannah and I ..."

"What? Happily ever after? Do fuck off. She was screwing another man."

"People get past worse."

"She was done with you, mate. I know you fucked her over, what with the mortgage and stuff, but, honestly, that was a gift to her. Made it so much easier."

"He beat her, Jessica. My brother. She didn't deserve that."

"No. She didn't. In that particular instance, Hannah was a victim. But she had you lined up anyway. And then she had Steve in her sights ... and soon enough it will be someone else. It's what she does. It's what she's always done."

"It's all bollocks, though, isn't it? It's all just stuff that we say. We're all unreliable narrators. Memories are written in code. Might as well shred them and stick them in the recycling for all the use they are. Compact them down with all the other rubbish. You should tell Tabitha that, see what she thinks."

"Perhaps I will." Tiny points of colour have formed at the top of her cheeks. The Prosecco bottle is empty, but she picks it up and puts it down again anyway. "How about us? First time around? Do you remember that? Has that all gone as well?"

"Ten weeks we were together. Nineteen dates, two weekends away. Just the one row, as far as I can recall."

"Okay. I'm flattered." She makes a face. "Am I flattered? How come ..."

"Because of shit like this," I say. "I couldn't forget you, Jessica."

"Such bullshit." Her smile is tentative. "Do you remember our first date? In that wine bar?"

"It was our second date."

"Was it? I suppose it was. Technically."

"I remember."

"What were we? Twenty three, twenty four?"

"Something like that."

"I mean, what the fuck were we doing? Children playing at being adults. With our Portishead and our red wine."

"It was white wine."

"Was it? Whatever. The stuff I told you. On our first date. Jesus."

"Like taking a shit, you said."

"I can't believe I said that."

"You really did."

"I'm much more refined now."

"So much more. It finished us. First time around. We couldn't take it, either of us. All that knowledge."

"I suppose not."

"I always wondered why you told me all that stuff. You barely knew me."

"I don't know. You had a nice face."

"I still do."

"This is true. The thing is, Nick, I trusted you."

"Jesus."

"Tell me, in all these years, have you ever repeated what I said? To Hannah, to Patrick? To anyone?"

"No. No, I haven't."

"Well then," she says.

Then my phone rings and for some reason I answer it.

Chapter 33

Of course my mother was there. She was on me before I'd closed the front door.

"And where were you last night? Some woman, I suppose. I can smell it on you."

I pushed past her and ran up the stairs. "None of your business."

"You could have called, at least. I was worried."

"We both know that's not true," I called down as I stuffed some essentials into a couple of holdalls.

"The way you talk to me. In my own house." The stairway is narrow and I had to turn sideways to carry both bags down the stairs. She watched me from the hallway. "What's this?"

"I'm staying with a friend for a bit."

"A friend? You don't have any friends. Not since Richard gave you the sack." After my win I'd quit my job with Richard. I'd told her that I'd been laid off, with a payment of sorts. Her words stung, though, as they were essentially true.

"You don't know how many friends I've got."

Her thin arms were folded across her chest. "How long is this nonsense going to last, then? I do need to know. I can't afford to buy for two if I don't need to."

"I'm not sure. I'll let you know."

I was at the door. She had her housecoat on. She smelled of antiseptic and cigarettes. Her head tilted a fraction. "This is something to do with Patrick, isn't it?"

I turned away from her as I grappled with the door. "Why on earth would it have anything to do with Patrick? I haven't even spoken to him since …"

"You can't look at me, can you, boy?"

I made my way to the car. I felt her eyes on me as I started the ignition. My cheeks burned as I drove away.

Instead of going straight back to Hannah's I parked on Unthank Road and visited my usual Ladbrokes. It was early and Ray was alone. His head dipped when he saw that it was me.

"I'm not here to have a bet," I said.

"Hallelujah."

"Look, Ray … can I tell you something?"

He looked at me warily. He stood propped against the counter, shirt sleeves rolled right up to the top of his arms. "That depends what it is." I hesitated. "I'm not a priest. This is not a confessional."

"Thanks for the clarification. I'd always wondered."

He sighed. "Go on then."

I told him about Hannah and Patrick. It came out in a rush.

"I see. And you're on your way round there now? With all your gear?"

"With some of it, at least." It suddenly occurred to me that I didn't need to go back for the rest of my possessions. I could buy anything I really needed. I could start again if I wanted to.

"You've been wanting to move out."

"This isn't how I planned it."

"Man makes plans, God laughs."

"I thought you said this wasn't a confessional?"

"You get the homespun wisdom for free."

"Thanks. Makes all the difference."

He made us a tea each and plonked them on the counter. "What you should be doing, of course, is going to the police."

"I can't."

"You can. You should."

"Not unless Hannah ..."

"It's Hannah that should be talking to someone, Nick. Not you."

"She came to me. She *needs* me."

"She needs help, Nick. After what she's been through."

"I'm trying ..."

"Professional help is what I mean."

I looked at my tea. I didn't drink any. A scummy film was forming on the surface. "I'm out of my depth."

"You're doing your best."

"Thanks, Ray."

"For what?"

"For listening. For making it seem real, at least. When I'm with Hannah, in that house – in *Patrick's* house – it's like some alternate reality. I can't get a handle on it."

"You care about her?"

"Of course I do. I *think* I do. I'm not sure it matters what I think."

"Well, as long as we're clear."

"Not a word, though, Ray. To anyone."

"We bookmakers are known for our discretion."

"I mean it."

"Who would I tell, Nick? Why would anyone care?"

He had a point.

*

Later Hannah made us chicken and salad and opened a bottle of wine. She asked how I'd got on with my mum and I told her. It didn't take long. She nodded but didn't say anything.

The locks had been changed, front and back. "These are yours," she said, handing me a set of keys. "There are locks on all of the windows now as well. The security guys are coming early tomorrow."

"I'll make myself scarce."

"You don't have to."

"I need to see Dan anyway."

"Okay." She took a tiny sip of wine. "You'll be back by evening, though? Just in case?"

"I will. Has he called today?"

"Just once. At lunchtime." She shrugged. "It was fine."

I pushed my plate away. "Sorry. Not very hungry. Shall we take the wine outside? It's a nice evening."

The garden was a small rectangle with a lawn and neat flowerbeds with a paved area next to patio doors. A pair of white cast iron chairs sat on the paving next to a matching table. We made ourselves comfortable and Hannah poured us some more wine. The air was warm and softening, scented with jasmine and apple blossom. Hannah ducked back into the living room and returned carrying her handbag.

She produced a cigarette from the bag. "I've got some left from the other day. Do you mind?"

"Of course not."

She lit it and blew a stream of smoke away from me. "Filthy habit."

"It doesn't suit you."

"It's dirty and stupid. I hate it. But it's only until … he's gone."

"You can't just wish him away."

She tilted her head towards me. Her eyes were hooded. "I rather think I can. I've got a solicitor all lined up. I've got new locks. I've got evidence. I've got you; my knight in shining armour."

"Please don't say that."

"I was joking, Nick." She drank some wine and took another pull on her cigarette. The smoke dissipated in the still air. "Well, mostly."

"I'm not sure what use I'll be."

"You're a rock. You're *my* rock. I just need you to … face him. I can't. I just can't. He won't *do* anything. Oh, he might rant and rave a bit, give the neighbours a show, but that's all. He'll realise quickly enough that if he does anything else, I'll ruin him."

"And that will be that."

"Yes. That will be that. And then I'll deal with the rest; my parents, Jessica, work. Us." She looked at the cigarette. "If Patrick caught me doing this, he'd kill me."

"Us?"

She dropped the cigarette onto the patio and ground it out beneath a heel. "I did love him once."

"You did?"

"I think I did."

"Why?"

"You know better than that, Nick."

"What do you mean?"

"Trying to explain all that chemical shit."

"Is that what love is?"

"Do you have a better explanation?" I shook my head. I was flustered and out of my depth again. I drank some more wine. I drained the glass. It wasn't enough. "What about you and Jessica?"

"What about us?"

"That was love, I assume?"

"I don't know. I don't think so. You'd have to ask Jessica."

"Perhaps I have."

"Well, then. I ..."

"I'm teasing, Nick."

"Teasing. Right." I tried to drain my glass again, although I knew it was empty.

"It's a distraction, that's all."

"A distraction. Teasing or love?"

"Either or," she said.

Patrick's car pulled into the drive early on Friday afternoon. The street was awash with sunlight. Patrick squinted against it as he got out of his car and saw me standing on the doorstep. He was unshaven. He wore a checked shirt that he hadn't buttoned properly. It seemed odd to me that he hadn't noticed. He walked towards me. "Nick? What are you doing here?"

"Fair warning," I said, in a voice that seemed distant and scarcely my own. "We're filming this."

"We?" He hesitated. His eyes scanned the windows, from the bottom to the top. "Where's Hannah?"

"She's inside. She's safe."

"Safe?" He came towards me then and shoved me to one side. I tried to stand my ground. My legs felt watery, my whole body seemed insubstantial, as though I was fading away. He pushed at the door. He started to drag his house keys out of a trouser pocket and then noticed the new lock. "What the fuck is this?"

His face was in mine. I smelled his breath and his animal scent. "New locks. All the windows, all the doors. Alarms. Cameras."

"Let me in." He rattled the door knob again. "Hannah," he shouted. "Let me the fuck in."

"I know what you did," I said.

His hand fell from the door and he moved very close. "You don't know anything." His arms were flexing, his hands balled into fists.

"Hit me, if you want. I will press charges."

"Don't think I won't."

"It wouldn't be the first time, would it? But now? I am a man, after all."

"The fuck you are. You're not a man. You don't know what a man is. You useless piece of piss." I watched the fury burn through him. His face contorted. He rocked backwards and forwards. I didn't back away.

"I know what you did," I said again. "I've seen it."

"You've seen it? That's cosy." His breathing slowed just a fraction.

"Hannah's got evidence; photos, film, recordings."

"Are you fucking my wife?" The anger was still there, but I could sense him swallowing it, forcing it down.

"She has a solicitor." I passed him a card. He snatched it from me, scanned it briefly then tossed it to the ground. "She suggests you get one too. You'll sign the house over to her. You'll leave her alone."

"Or what?"

"She goes to the police. And the pictures, the evidence, go everywhere; to everyone you know or have ever known. Mum, the neighbours, all over social media."

"She wouldn't do that."

"She would. I think you know she would."

"This is my house."

"Not any more. You messed up, Patrick. You've gone too far."

"This is none of your business."

"You're my brother …"

"I'm not your brother."

"You're my brother and I love you …"

He took a step back. He looked as though I'd slapped him. "Fuck off."

"But you disgust me. What you did disgusts me."

He moved away from the door and back towards his car. He rubbed both hands across his face and through his short hair. I heard the scrape of his stubble. "Does she know about the gambling? Does she know you're an addict, a degenerate?"

"If you come back in an hour your stuff will be on the front lawn. Most of it, anyway. We'll sort the rest out, bit by bit. But you won't see Hannah. You won't speak to her."

"You're a cuckoo," he said. "A cuckoo in the fucking nest."

"We'll record everything. Anytime you're near this house it'll be on film."

He was at his car by now. The couple at the house opposite were in their front garden, watching. I saw movement at other nearby windows, as well, and it was clear that Patrick did too. He opened the door. "You're dead. To me, to mum. You don't even have a name. You never existed."

I folded my arms and waited for him to leave. He did eventually. As Hannah said, he had no choice. I stood for a moment after his car had pulled away, in the silence, stunned, lost in an adrenaline hum. The sun was too bright. My thoughts were burning, adrift. Then I heard Hannah, unlocking the door from the inside. She tugged me into the cool of the hallway. I was shaking. She held me and I felt the warmth of her breath against my face and neck.

Chapter 34

It's my mother's landline that comes up on the screen, but the voice that punches into my ear is Patrick's. "You've got to get here, man."

"Patrick? What the ..."

"It was an accident. I mean, she went for me. I don't under ... look, just get here. Now."

I start to say something else but the line is dead. I try to call back and I get the engaged tone.

"What?" Jessica says.

"It's Patrick. He called from mum's. Something's wrong. I've got to get over there."

Jessica stands. "I'll drive you."

"You've been drinking. It's fine. I'll walk."

"But ..."

"It won't take me long. Honestly, it's for the best."

"Call then. Let me know what's going on?"

"Of course."

She gives me a brief hug and then I leave.

The evening is cold and still, but I barely feel it. I half-walk and half-run and within twenty minutes I am at my mother's familiar front door.

I say my brother's name as I enter. The house is dark except for a puddle of light emanating from the kitchen. As I push the door open I see my mother. She's lying on her back next to the kitchen door. She's wearing her usual green housecoat. Her legs are together, bent at the knees, her arms are splayed like the branches of a tree, above her head, which is canted, at an angle to the left. A heavy, black wrought-iron door stop, shaped like an anvil, is next to her head. Blood is smeared across its surface. There's blood on the floor, too, and a wine-like dribble of it oozes from my mother's left ear.

My brother sits at the kitchen table. He has a large knife in his right hand. He points it towards his heart. I recognise the knife; I remember my mother brandishing it over Christmas dinner a few months earlier.

"Have you called an ambulance?"

Patrick registers my presence for the first time. "She came for me, Nick. She was so angry. I just gave her a little push, that's all ..."

"Have you called an ambulance?"

"No point." His voice is thin, defeated. His face is shrouded by a shrubby, disparate beard that looks as though it belongs on another face entirely.

I kneel next to my mother and place my fingers on her throat and then her wrist. Her flesh is slack and cool. Her eyes are closed, but her mouth hangs half-open. Her false teeth are slightly askew. She wouldn't like that, I think, but I don't know what to do about it.

"Why would she do that? Why would she come for me?" He breaks into a protracted, meaty cough that seems to occupy and flex every part of his body. "Fuck's sake," he says, when it finally finishes.

"Where have you been, Patrick?"

"Kicked me out, didn't they? Bastards. Couldn't pay the rent. I've been on the streets. King's Lynn and then here. It's so cold. So fucking cold. Do you know what it took for me to come back here? Do you know what it cost me?" He won't look at me and he won't look at our mother, either, so his eyes go to odd places: the ceiling, the kettle, the painting of a bowl of cherries that hangs on the far wall. "And then she goes for me. Silly old ..."

"I spoke to Ivy."

"Ivy? What were you doing speaking to Ivy?"

"I was looking for you."

"You were looking for me? Nick? You looked for me?" He sees me now. His eyes are liquid, wide open, the whites threaded with grey and red. He looks broken and hollowed out and I want to hold him. I also want to help him push the knife into his heart, just to get it over with.

"Ivy told me about ... the past. The stuff you said to her, about mum, her family."

"How is she? Ivy?"

"She's okay. We're looking after her."

"We?"

"Me and Jessica."

"Jessica, huh?" A congested chuckle, the merest hint of the old Patrick, gone in an instant. "You told mum, yeah? About what Ivy said? Why would you do that?"

"I had to know."

"Why? What good did it do? I was protecting you."

"Why did you tell Ivy?"

"I had to tell someone. I liked Ivy. She was ... maybe mum could've been like that. Do you think?" I shrug, I've got no idea what I'm meant to say. "It was locked in my head all those years. I had to get it out. Look up Flossenbürg, if you really want to know. They hung some of them. The guards. Not all, but some." He points to the cooling body opposite. "I didn't need to look it up. She told me it all. Over and over. Just me. Not even dad. Just me. I was special, she said. I could take it. I'd understand."

"Dad didn't know?"

"Dad was weak. Ineffectual. Like you."

"We've got to call anyway; an ambulance, the police. We can't just leave her there."

He looks at our mother. He coughs again, more briefly this time. "It was just a little push. To get her off me. Stupid, stupid."

"I'm making the call, Patrick."

"Just give me an hour."

"What? Why?"

"An hour. That's all. I beat my wife and killed my mother. We know how this ends for me. Fuck's sake, it's already ended. Just an hour, that's all. You owe me that."

"I owe you?"

"You took Hannah. You took my house. I protected you, Nick."

"You hit me. You told Ivy I was dead."

"Is there anything to drink in this place? Apart from sherry. Get me some whisky, Nick. Get me some whisky and give me an hour."

I find an unopened bottle of Teachers in a cupboard in the living room. I place it in front of Patrick. He looks at it but doesn't move. I'm not entirely sure that he is capable of movement. His eyes are deep set and hollow. The flesh on his face and hands is pared tight to the bone.

"I'll get you a glass."

"I don't need a glass." He is completely still, his eyes on the bottle.

I kneel by my mother again. Her housecoat has gathered at the waist and I pull at the material in tiny, fussy tugs until the surface is smooth. Even in death I am cowed by her presence. I feel reduced, a child again. Less than a child. I stand and look at my brother and it is as though he is barely there either. I wonder if we just remain here, the two of us, if we wait and wait, then when they finally come, they will find only our mother's body alongside two pathetic puddles of clothing.

I move to my brother's side. He remains motionless and doesn't speak. As I ease past him I grip his shoulder lightly. Through his old leather jacket and his sweater and shirt I can feel only bone.

I walk through the hallway towards the front door. It takes an astonishingly long time. It is very dark. I am accompanied by shadows and ghosts. I see a suggestion of moonlight through the cut glass semi-circle set into the top of the door.

I open the door and close it quickly behind me. The sky is mint-black, studded with stars. I take a deep lungful of the cold, dark air. It feels heady, narcotic.

I pull my phone from my pocket and call Jessica.

ABOUT THE AUTHOR

Andrew Humphrey is the author of two collections of short stories, both published by Elastic Press. *Open The Box* appeared in 2002 and *Other Voices*, which was one of the winners of the inaugural East Anglian Book Award, in 2008. His debut novel, *Alison,* was published by TTA Press also in 2008. Described as *East Anglia's laureate of loss and alienation,* Andrew's short fiction has appeared in *Crimewave, Midnight Street, Black Static* and *The Third Alternative*. He lives and works in Norwich and has a reluctant presence on Twitter (@andyhumphrey11). As well as *Debris*, Head Shot Press have also recently published his third short story collection, *A Punch To The Heart*.